Praise for Gail Gaymer Martin

"Gail Gaymer Martin has certainly mastered the art of creating romantic tension between characters."
—Carly Kendall, www.carlybirdshome.blogspot.com, on *A Dad of His Own*

"A fun read with a serious side."
—*RT Book Reviews* on *Bride in Training*

"Faith, hope, love and forgiveness all play a role in this terrifically warm, endearing tale."
—*RT Book Reviews* on *Family in His Heart*

Praise for Brenda Minton

"A lovely romance where the characters' acceptance of God's plans surprisingly brings them their hearts' desires."
—*RT Book Reviews* on *The Cowboy's Family*

"A satisfyingly emotional story."
—*RT Book Reviews* on *The Cowboy's Courtship*

"Brenda Minton excels at showing readers deep and intense emotions. This is a powerful story of... recognizing what is truly important in life."
—Debbie Wiley, www.bookilluminations.com, on *Jenna's Cowboy Hero*

GAIL GAYMER MARTIN

A former counselor, Gail Gaymer Martin is an award-winning author, writing women's fiction, romance and romance suspense for Love Inspired Books and Barbour Publishing. This book is her forty-fifth published novel and she has more than three million books in print. Gail is the author of twenty-seven worship resource books and *Writing the Christian Romance,* released by Writers Digest Books. She is a cofounder of American Christian Fiction Writers, the premier Christian fiction organization in the country.

When not writing, Gail enjoys traveling, presenting workshops at writers' conferences, speaking at churches and libraries, as well as singing as a soloist, praise leader and choir member at her church, where she also plays handbells and handchimes. Gail also sings with one of the finest Christian chorales in Michigan, the Detroit Lutheran Singers. She is a lifelong resident of Michigan and lives with her husband, Bob, in the Detroit suburbs. Visit her website at www.gailmartin.com. Write to Gail at P.O. Box 760063, Lathrup Village, MI, 48076 or at authorgailmartin@aol.com. She enjoys hearing from readers.

BRENDA MINTON

started creating stories to entertain herself during hour-long rides on the school bus. In high school she wrote romance novels to entertain her friends. The dream grew and so did her aspirations to become an author. She started with notebooks, handwritten manuscripts and characters that refused to go away until their stories were told. Eventually she put away the pen and paper and got down to business with the computer. The journey took a few years, with some encouragement and rejection along the way—as well as a lot of stubbornness on her part. In 2006, her dream to write for Love Inspired Books came true. Brenda lives in the rural Ozarks with her husband, three kids and an abundance of cats and dogs. She enjoys a chaotic life that she wouldn't trade for anything—except, on occasion, a beach house in Texas. You can stop by and visit at her website, www.brendaminton.net.

CHRISTMAS GIFTS
Gail Gaymer Martin
Brenda Minton

Love Inspired

Recycling programs for this product may not exist in your area.

LOVE INSPIRED BOOKS

ISBN-13: 978-0-373-81584-5

CHRISTMAS GIFTS

Copyright © 2011 by Harlequin Books S.A.

The publisher acknowledges the copyright holders of the individual works as follows:

SMALL TOWN CHRISTMAS
Copyright © 2011 by Gail Gaymer Martin

HER CHRISTMAS COWBOY
Copyright © 2011 by Brenda Minton

www.LoveInspiredBooks.com

Printed in U.S.A.

CONTENTS

SMALL TOWN CHRISTMAS   7
Gail Gaymer Martin

HER CHRISTMAS COWBOY   147
Brenda Minton

SMALL TOWN CHRISTMAS

Gail Gaymer Martin

Thanks to Love Inspired Books Senior Editor, Melissa Endlich, who invited me to participate in this special two-in-one Christmas novel. Many thanks to the wonderful people I met while visiting the real town of Harrisville. Thanks to the principal of Alcona Elementary School, Mrs. Sharon Fairchild, and her staff, including a second-grade teacher. To Manny Pompa, owner of the Flour Garden, who provided me with information about the Christmas tree lighting event and Christmas in the Village. To Judy Labadie with the Harrisville Chamber of Commerce, who answered many of my questions in person and via the telephone. To Carol Luck, head librarian at the Alcona County Library in Harrisville, and to Deidre Gray, owner of Maggies On Main, who fielded many questions or guided me to someone who knew the answer. As always, my love and thanks to my husband, Bob, who stands by me even with my last-minute research plans.

You have made known to me the paths of life;
you will fill me with joy in your presence.
—*Acts* 2:28

"Whatever happens, this works well for us."

Chapter One

"You do understand that this is only temporary?"

Amy Carroll jerked her eyes away from the fall scene outside the window and gazed at the Alcona Elementary School principal. "Yes, I understand, Mrs. Fredericks. My grandmother told me the situation when she called." Grams seemed to know everything in the small town. "Temporary is fine. I lived in Chicago for five years, and I would miss the hustle and bustle being gone too long. I'd love to be called back, but I don't expect it to happen."

"Don't give up hope. You might be."

The finality washed over her. "They've closed a number of schools in the Chicago area, including the one where I taught. My only option would be finding a position somewhere outside the city."

Mrs. Fredericks smacked her hands together. "Whatever happens, this works well for us. You have excellent credentials, and I'm pleased you'll be joining our staff on Monday to finish out the school year." She closed the file folder, slipped it into her desk tray and rolled back in her chair. "Welcome to Alcona Elementary." She rose and extended her hand. "The secretary will give you what you need— a school calendar, your textbooks and a lesson planning guide. You've taught second grade before, so it's perfect."

Amy stood and grasped her hand. "It is, and thanks so much." She gave a firm shake and stepped toward the door. "I look forward to—"

"Mrs. Fredericks." The office secretary leaned into the room. "Mr. Russet—you know, the twins' father—is waiting to see you."

"The twins. Yes." A heavy sigh whisked the air as the principal's shoulders slumped. "You can..." She paused and eyed Amy. "Ask him to wait just a moment."

Amy took another step toward the door, anxious to retreat.

"Please wait a moment, Miss Carroll."

Amy jerked to a halt.

"The twins will be in your class next week."

"Really?" Amy tried to keep a smile on her face.

Mrs. Fredericks nodded. "It might help you to meet the girls. They have a propensity for getting into trouble. Earlier this week, Holly tripped Ivy while she was jumping rope."

Amy struggled to keep her eyebrows from arching. "Is this common?"

"I'm afraid so. It's their typical behavior, and as always, Holly insisted it was only an accident."

"Could it have been?" She liked to give children the benefit of the doubt in such situations.

"Not usually, but I think sometimes Ivy sets up the situation. Almost feeds Holly the ideas. Their teacher hasn't put her finger on the trouble. Maybe you can."

Maybe you can. Amy managed to keep her composure. The pressure didn't set well, although the comment appeared to be a compliment. But what if she failed?

"I'd like you to meet them. They're right across the hall in the cafeteria. It might help you prepare for Monday."

A niggling sense of worry settled over Amy. "I suppose that would be…practical."

"Plus you can keep an eye on them while I talk with their father." Mrs. Fredericks chuckled and motioned her to follow. "Let me introduce you."

Amy followed Mrs. Fredericks through the doorway. Across the hall, she spotted the girls seated on each side of the cafeteria benches, cuter and sweeter looking than her perception. Although not identical twins, their features were similar. Their bright blue eyes, like the Caribbean sea, widened when they saw the principal.

The child with a tawny-colored ponytail swung her legs over the bench. "It wasn't me, Mrs. Fredericks."

"Yes, it was." The blonder twin slipped from her seat, her hair gathered into a ponytail on each side of her head. "Mrs. Fredericks, Holly tore up my drawing in art class."

"I know. Please sit for a moment." Holly gestured to the benches. "I want you to meet someone."

Their heads turned and they scrutinized Amy before eyeing each other, a hint of fear quickly covered by determination.

Amy's heart squeezed.

"Miss Carroll, this young lady is Holly." She rested her hand on the one with honey-brown hair and the deep frown. "And this is Ivy."

Ivy gazed at her, curiosity written on her face.

Amy stepped closer. "Hi. It's nice to meet you."

Neither responded.

Mrs. Fredericks eyed them. "Miss Carroll will be your new teacher, starting Monday."

"New teacher?" Holly's ponytail flipped as she swiveled toward Amy.

"Remember?" Mrs. Fredericks leaned forward, resting her palms on the table. "Mrs. Larch is expecting a baby soon, so she's taking a leave."

Their intent expression flickered as their glances collided. "She told us." Their responses blended in agreement.

"Good. Now I'll leave you with Miss Carroll, and you can have a nice talk." She turned to Amy. "I'll be back shortly." Mrs. Fredericks offered a pleasant grin, then strode toward the door. Before she exited she glanced over her shoulder. "When I return, I'll introduce you to the girls' father. I'm sure you'd like that."

"Our dad?" two voices rang in unison.

Amy wasn't so sure she was ready to meet her first parent quite yet, but she clenched her teeth and agreed. When she looked at the twins, they were peering at her again, Holly with her arms crossed at her chest and Ivy with one fist jammed into her waist.

Amy pulled her gaze upward, reading the signs written in large black letters that hung above the tables. Citizenship. Responsibility. Apparently, the twins hadn't read them. She bit the inside of her lip. Every year she'd met children and their parents, but today the meeting seemed more like confrontation.

"Why are you here?"

Holly's blunt question grabbed Amy's attention. She held back a grin. That's the question she'd planned to ask them. Instead she slipped around the end of the bench and sat at the table. Both girls scrutinized her before they settled down again, their query still hanging on the air.

"I came to pick up the textbooks used in your class," she answered simply. Getting to know the two girls better seemed more important than showing her authority. Still, behind those sweet faces, Amy sensed that some kind of unhappiness or hurt was dredging up their troublesome behavior. She looked from one girl to the other. "I think the more important question is what are *you* doing here?" She swung her arm toward the cafeteria serving counter.

"Mrs. Fredericks made us sit here."

"Hmm?" Amy tapped her finger against her cheek. "I wonder why? It's not lunch time."

Ivy bit her lip. "Kids who misbehave have to sit in here and wait."

Holly's frown deepened. "I didn't do anything bad."

Ivy rested her palms on the table, pressing her face closer to Holly's, her look searing through her sister. "You tore up my drawing."

"But you said it wasn't any good."

Ivy fell back to her seat. "If I wanted to tear it up, I would have done it."

"That's right, Ivy." Amy focused on Holly, monitoring her tone. "When something belongs to me, I make decisions about what to do with it. No one else."

Holly turned her head toward the doorway and tightened her ponytail.

Amy didn't respond to the child's behavior. "What kind of pictures were you drawing?"

Holly's head tilted back, as if she wasn't sure Amy really cared.

Hoping to soothe the tension, Amy grinned. "I'd like to hear about what you do in the classroom because I'll be your new teacher on Monday."

Holly's shoulders relaxed. "We were drawing pictures of pilgrims and Indians for our social studies."

"Because it's almost Thanksgiving, right?" Amy gave them a wink.

"Uh-huh, and…" A movement by the door caught her attention.

"Daddy!" Both girls shot from the benches and ran to a harried-looking man who stood inside the doorway, his hands tucked in his jacket pockets.

Amy's heart gave a twinge. A five o'clock shadow encompassed his lean jaw and his chestnut hair was tousled as if he'd run his fingers through it many times. His eyebrows stretched above his caramel brown eyes, flashing with emotion. She couldn't tell if he were ready to blow a gasket or just fizzle.

Her question was answered when he released a nervous laugh and rocked on his heels. "You must be Miss Carroll, the new teacher." He strode toward her. "I'm the girls' father." He wiped his hand on his pant leg before extending it to Amy.

Amy met him halfway while the twins hovered at his side. She dropped her palm into his, aware of his warm grip.

"Nice to meet you." His frustration couldn't hide behind his pleasant expression.

"Good to meet you, too, Mr. Russet."

Behind him Mrs. Fredericks watched the scene with seeming interest. "I'll leave you now. And I'll see you on Monday, Miss Carroll." She gave her a wave and vanished.

When she looked back, Amy saw the girls cringe,

and her skin prickled. "Your daughters were telling me about their social studies."

"Social studies? Really?" A grin played on his lips before his gaze dropped to the twins. "You know, girls, we have some serious talking to do."

The twins lowered their eyes, but in them, she saw consternation. Maybe remorse. Whatever it was, the look caught her attention.

When she looked up, their father was studying her with curiosity. "I'm sure we've met."

Amy drew back. "Met? Where?"

"At your grandmother's. Years ago."

She did a double take. "My grandmother's?"

A crooked smile curved his mouth. "Ellie Carroll. Lake Street. Right?"

"Yes, that's it." But Amy's memory drew a blank.

"We live on Lake Street, too." The twins' voices melded together.

His grin widened. "I thought you'd remember. It was maybe eleven years ago."

Her face knotted as she tried to recall. "I don't think so." Yet something shimmered in the shadow of her mind. "I was only eighteen then, Mr. Russet."

"I was twenty-three, earning money as a handyman while I looked for a job." He grinned. "Maybe you remember my first name, Mike?"

Amy gasped in surprise, as the memory came flooding back.

"You're the guy who dug out Grams's old shrubbery and planted new ones." She pictured him in the summer sun, his muscles flexing while his shirt hung on her grandmother's deer ornament in the tree-sheltered yard.

"The same, except a few pounds heavier and some wrinkles."

Amy studied his face, seeing only a few worry lines. His unruly hair hadn't changed. She remembered how it ruffled in the breeze, his lean handsome face taut with concentration. They were young then, and she'd flirted with him. But when she went inside, her grandmother had notified her he was newly married. Heat rose up Amy's neck at the thought. She hoped he didn't remember she'd toyed with him.

She managed to look at him. "I'll tell Grams I saw you."

"Gramma Ellie sits with us."

Amy's head turned toward Ivy. "She does?"

"Quite often, actually." Mike shrugged a shoulder. "She and the girls get on great."

Even though she tried to listen to what he was saying, her memory kept flashing back to the summer they'd first met. Her chest pressed against her lungs, the same reaction she had that day. But today Grams's words rang clear, and she knew better. He was married. Amy eyed the doorway, calculating how she might whip past the beguiling man and escape. She came to her senses and checked her watch. "Speaking of Grams, I'd better be on my way. She's expecting me home, and I don't want her to worry."

"Certainly, Miss Carroll." He stepped aside, his

gaze settling on the girls. "I have a couple things to take care of myself."

"Nice to meet you, Holly and Ivy. I'll see you on Monday."

Ivy gave a wave, but Holly only sent her a questioning look.

"And nice to meet you...again." She could only glance at Mike, fearing he would notice he'd flustered her just as he had that day long ago. She hurried through the doorway, wishing Mrs. Russet had been the one to face the principal about the girls.

Discomfort followed her to her car, and after she opened the door, she turned and slammed it closed. Too busy dealing with her memories, she'd forgotten to pick up the textbooks and lesson plan book in the front office.

Quickly darting into the building, Amy gathered the materials from the secretary. Safe outside, she slipped into her hatchback and headed down Highway 72 toward town. She loved working with children, and although she knew the twins might be a problem, she decided to formulate a plan of action. If she had solutions before the problems occurred, she might be able to teach the girls a little about cooperation and getting along. Being an only child, she'd never experienced a sister's relationship firsthand, but that wouldn't stop her from trying to help the girls with theirs.

Mike's frustration inched into her mind. He seemed at a loss on how to deal with them, which made her assume the twins' mother did most of the disciplining. If she talked with Mrs. Russet, perhaps they could decide how best to resolve the twins' issues.

Reaching Main Street, she stopped at the Local IGA and picked up the groceries her grandmother had asked her to bring home. When she turned down Lake Street, she looked closely at each residence, curious to know which might be the Russets'.

Soon she turned into her grandmother's driveway, washed by its homey feeling. She'd spent so many summers at Grams's, listening to her stories and learning how to bake cookies. Her grandmother taught her so many things she'd missed living in Illinois with her dad. And spending Christmas with her grandmother made her smile.

As soon as her car came to a halt in the long driveway, Grams's face appeared at the kitchen window. Amy waved before lifting the bags and heading inside. "Sorry I'm late. I hope you didn't need the groceries."

"No, they're for tomorrow."

"Good." She set the sacks on the kitchen table. "The principal wanted me to meet two sisters who'll be in my class. They'd gotten into trouble, and—"

"Holly and Ivy." Her rosy cheeks lifted in a grin. "Am I right?"

Amy chuckled. "You are." She pulled milk and eggs from the package and set them in the refrigerator. "And I talked with their dad."

"Poor Mike." Grams shook her head. "That man has faced the principal more than he did when he was in school, I'm sure." She lifted the bag of flour. "Those little darlings are so needy, but you'd be surprised how good they are with me."

"Their dad told me." Amy tried to picture the girls' expressions without defiance and questioning looks. "I assume their mother works. I wish she'd been the one—"

Grams shook her head. "Their mother died a few years ago."

"Died? That's awful."

"I think the twins were about four years old. Mike's raising those girls alone."

Amy's heart wrenched. She knew what that was like. When her own mother ran off without taking her along, her father had tried so hard to be both father and mother for her.

Grams reached over and patted her hand. "I knew you'd understand, but you were always a good girl. Never had an ounce of worry for you." She shrugged. "Each person's different."

Her grandmother's words didn't console her. Yes, she'd been good, but it didn't change how she'd felt. Most girls needed a mom. Even having her precious grandmother couldn't make up for the loss of a mother. And she'd watched her father suffer and grow distant without realizing how it had affected her. Romance and marriage stuck in her mind like a thorn. Who wanted to get involved in the fickle emotions of love?

Amy folded the grocery bags while Mike's image stayed in her mind. Twin girls. No wife. A job. Household responsibilities. That wasn't a life for anyone. As the truth struck her, one of the sacks she'd folded slipped from her hands. She bent to retrieve it, facing the fact that her own life was much too similar to Mike's, but without children. Work. Errands. A few friends. Not much.

Had Mike been able to overcome the pain of his wife's death? Her stomach tightened as her gaze drifted to her grandmother. She swallowed the questions. If she asked, Grams would either make something out of her curiosity or warn her off, just as she'd done eleven years ago.

What was the sudden attraction to a widower and two troubled girls? She'd passed up plenty of dates more than once. Just the thought of getting involved with someone made as much sense as living in a small town. She couldn't do it for an extended time. Not for a million dollars.

Chapter Two

Mike pulled up to his house, priding himself on keeping his cool with the twins while they were still at school. But how much longer could he cope with it? Even though his daughters were precious to him, they were stretching him to the limit.

He turned off the ignition and veiled his frustration. "Inside, girls." He swung open the door and slammed it, his first action that showed his real feelings.

The girls' voices whiffled past him as they darted toward the house. He searched for the front door key, but instead of hurrying ahead, he gazed down the street to the large house with the wide stone porch. He couldn't help but grin despite his stress.

His mind flew back to the day he'd met Amy Carroll. Ellie had spoken about her so often. She'd been a lovely young girl, full of energy and fresh as dew. She'd flirted with him, and when he returned home, he'd told Laura and they'd laughed.

He headed to his porch, but his thoughts clung to Amy. Her long brown hair, the color of ripe chestnuts, hung in a slight wave, and her cinnamon-colored eyes had widened when he'd mentioned their first meeting. Color had spotted her cheeks, letting him know she'd remembered the details of that day.

Bounding up the porch steps, he pulled his attention back to the girls. What would he do with them now? Nothing seemed to work. He stuck the key in the lock and then focused for a moment on each twin.

Ivy leaned against him as she tended to do, but belligerence heightened in Holly's eyes.

When he pushed the door back, she whipped past him while Ivy lingered, wanting to plead her case, he was sure.

"Daddy, I didn't do anything. Holly ripped my—"

"I know what happened. Mrs. Fredericks gave me all the details, including a few other incidents that they didn't call me in for." He motioned toward her bedroom. "Change your clothes, and we'll talk."

She slogged toward her room, her face covered by the wounded look he'd come to know.

He dropped onto a kitchen chair and pressed his face into his hands. He'd made mistakes. He'd spoiled the girls. When their mother died, he'd been lost. But later he was determined to be a father and mother to them. Impossible, he realized now. Instead of guiding them, he'd pampered them and let their misbe-havior go unchecked. No more.

His head ached, and he dug his fists into his eyes willing the pain away. When he lifted his head to the sunshine streaming through the window, the throb remained.

The previous teacher, Mrs. Larch, hadn't been able to control the girls. They'd continued to distract the class. He was exhausted and out of ideas on how best to control his girls. If only Laura hadn't died, maybe then— He shook his head. Why hadn't he realized how sick she was?

Regret was useless. If he clung to all of his what-ifs, he would live in the past forever. Moving forward with his life needed to happen now, not only for his sake but for the girls'. He massaged the cords in his neck to ease the tension.

Amy slipped into his mind, bringing him hope. Until she'd noticed him, he'd watched her talking to the girls when he'd crossed the hall to the cafeteria. The twins were listening to her, and even though Holly's belligerence still marred her pretty face, so like her mother's, Ivy seemed to hang on to her every word. How had she done it? He slapped the tabletop and rose. That's what he needed to do. See if Amy could teach him something. Discipline with love. Could he learn to do that?

Mike slipped off his jacket, hung it on the back of a chair and strode to the refrigerator. He poured a slosh of milk and swallowed, still feeling a hungering void.

Noise from the hall caught his attention. He rinsed the glass and set it in the sink while his gaze drifted down the street to Ellie's tree-filled property. An unfamiliar car sat at the back of the driveway, a sporty hatchback, practical but spirited, with its deep orange color. No doubt Amy had returned home.

"Daddy."

He turned, startled by Ivy's voice. The two girls stood beside the table, waiting. "Let's sit in the living room, okay?" He didn't wait for an answer. He marched into the room and settled into his recliner. The girls plopped onto the sofa.

"I'm hungry, so don't take long."

Holly's sarcastic tone grated him, but he bit his tongue, unwilling to argue. "I don't want to know what happened today because Mrs. Fredericks told me. I want to know what we'll do about it."

"About what?" Ivy's wide eyes sent him an innocent gaze.

"About your behavior." He monitored his tone.

"If Holly wouldn't tear up my—"

Mike held up his hand to shush her. "This isn't about a picture or being tripped when you jumped rope or anything else." He aimed his gaze at Holly. "This has to do with making changes. I'm tired of being called up to school. Do you realize I have to take time off from work to come there and listen to the same old stories about your behavior?"

"But—"

"I want solutions, Holly, not *buts*."

Ivy started to titter, and Holly soon followed.

He stared at them and waited for their silliness to end. He'd hoped to reason with them, to find some solutions. Mrs. Fredericks had given him one, and although he'd negated it, the idea might set a fire under the girls.

"Sorry, Daddy, but you said—"

"I know what I said, Ivy. I'm asking for changes. What will they be?"

The two gazed at the floor, their hands in their laps, and said nothing.

"Then I have a solution. Mrs. Fredericks recommends that we split the two of you into different second grade classes."

"No, Daddy. Please." Ivy's volume rose with each word.

His mind reeled. "Why not? I would think you'd be happy."

She shook her head in high speed. "We need to be together."

"Why?" His focus shifted from one to the other. "Together isn't working, so why?"

"Because we're all we got."

Hearing Ivy knocked him backward. *We're all we got.* His heart wrenched. He leaned forward, his elbows resting on his thighs. "Then you will make some changes in your behavior, or it will be out of my hands."

A frown crept to their faces.

"Will Mrs. Fredericks make us go to different classes?"

Ivy's plaintive look stymied him. "If you keep causing problems, then I think she will."

She shifted toward Holly, who'd said little. "Do you want to go to another class?"

Holly looked away with a faint shake of the head.

Mike remained silent, giving them time to think until both pairs of eyes returned to his. "You have the weekend to make a decision." And he had the weekend to figure out what to do. "Remember what I said." He rose. "By the way, Holly, if you're hungry, eat some fruit. Dinner won't be for a while yet."

They popped up and sped from the room while he sat questioning his threat. If they separated during school, would it make a difference? What about their behavior at home? His chest constricted while Ivy's words rang in this head. *We're all we got.* He needed to understand what she meant.

The refrigerator door opened, and before it closed, he rose and headed into the kitchen. "If you want to watch TV, you can, but I know you have some homework today. Mrs. Fredericks told me."

"Can we do it tomorrow?"

Holly's favorite question rang in his ears. "You're going to spend part of the day with Gramma Ellie. Do you want to do homework then?"

"No." Ivy spun on her heel. "I'll do mine now. I'd rather have fun tomorrow."

Holly gave it some thought before she followed Ivy toward her room.

Mike headed into the kitchen, pulled out an apple and took a bite. Dinner was more than an hour away, and for once, he had time on his hands.

Leaves drifting past the window caught his eye. He planned to rake them tomorrow, but his body charged with energy. His gaze drifted and he spotted Amy in Ellie's front yard tugging leaves toward the side lot. Big yard. Big job for a slender woman.

He slipped on his jacket, but before he stepped outside, he ambled to the twins' bedroom doors. "I'm going out to rake. I'll be there if you need me."

A muffled okay came from Ivy's room. Holly's was silent. She'd probably fallen asleep.

Mike stepped onto the side porch and grabbed his work gloves and rake, then headed down the steps. But instead of tackling his task, he strode across the street, drawn by the lithe woman whose opinion he valued.

When she spotted him, she stopped and leaned on the rake handle. Her hair shone with streaks of dark gold in the afternoon sun, and her cheeks were rosy with the crisp breeze. "So that's where you live. The blue-and-white house."

"Not too far away."

"It's cute. I admired it when I passed by earlier."

"Thanks." He'd never considered the house cute,

as she called it, but it motivated him to turn and take another look. "My wife picked the color. She loved blue."

Amy's smile faded. "I'm sorry about your loss. Grams told me."

He suspected Ellie had. He motioned to the lawn to change the subject. "Let me help you."

She shook her head. "You have your own leaves to take care of. I can—"

"I'm sure you can, but I'd like to help." He swung out the rake and gave a tug. The debris tangled in the tines, jerking him to a sudden stop. "Does Ellie... does your grandmother have an old sheet or maybe a tarp? We can make fast work of this if she does."

"A sheet?"

"We'll rake the leaves onto it and drag the load to the side. Much easier."

Her eyebrows arched. "That's a great idea." She dropped the rake. "Wish I'd thought of that a half hour ago."

She darted off as he watched her long legs make short work of the distance. A runner. He could picture her jogging down the streets of Chicago, turning heads as she went. The woman definitely turned his. Even though a tinge of guilt swept past him, he didn't let it sway his thoughts. Laura had been gone three years, and it had been a long time since he'd really looked at another woman.

Amy waved a white cloth at him as she returned. "Grams said to use this." She tossed it to him as she approached, a grin growing on her face. "Here's the deal. You help me, and I'll come over and help you."

Normally he wouldn't consider it, but for the first time in years, he felt like a man instead of just a dad. "Deal."

Together they spread the sheet on the grass and raked the leaves into the center. When it had filled they dragged the burden to the side lot. The trip repeated over and over, and before he realized how much time had passed, the twins were scuttling across the road.

"We're hungry." Ivy's softer voice reached him.

Holly's command followed. "It's time for dinner. Are you going to feed us?"

Mike checked his watch. Six o'clock. Time had flown. He eyed Ellie's yard, almost empty of leaves, and drew up his shoulders. "Appears I'm being summoned." He lifted the rake. "I can finish this tomorrow after work if you—"

"Tomorrow's your yard. This is all but done." She gave them a wave. "Your dad has been kind enough to help me with the leaves."

The twins spun toward the pile as if they hadn't noticed it. A grin grew on their faces, and before Mike could move, they'd darted past them toward the mound. Holly dived toward the heap first, but Ivy shot past and Holly tripped over her foot. She skidded onto her knees and tumbled into the crackling leaves as Ivy plowed in beside her, leaves flying into the air and skittering across the grass. Mike dropped his rake and dashed forward, but not before Holly was on top of her sister, hands around her throat. "You tripped me on purpose."

"No, she didn't." Mike grasped her jacket and yanked her up. "You tripped over her foot."

Tears flowed down Holly's face, more from his taking Ivy's side than from being hurt, he suspected.

"Are you okay?" Amy reached their side but stood back observing the fray.

As Mike pulled Ivy from the leaves, she gave him her sad-eyes look and rubbed her neck. "She choked me."

"I know." Embarrassed and helpless, he raked his fingers through his hair. "I'd better get these girls home."

Amy stepped closer. "If they're hungry, Grams is ordering pizza and—"

"Pizza!"

Apparently the argument had been forgotten, but their eager voices failed to influence him. "Thanks anyway, Amy."

"Daddy, I'm hungry." Holly's narrowed eyes matched her frown.

"Please don't bark at me." He turned a scowl back at her. "I'm sorry. The time flew and I didn't realize—" He sucked in air and stopped apologizing. That was it. He'd grown tired of marching to Holly's commands. "We'll go home and have dinner after we talk again."

"But the pizza." Her frown deepened.

Ivy leaned her head against his side. He wrapped his arm around her, pleased she'd not gotten mouthy, too.

Amy stepped back, looking uneasy. "I'll see you tomorrow."

"Tomorrow?" His response faded as his mind filled in the blanks. To rake leaves. "In the afternoon. I have to work in the morning."

"Afternoon's fine." A grin followed.

"Working Saturday happens on occasion." He gave a shrug and put on a smile. "Thanks for the pizza invitation, but..." He tilted his head toward the girls.

"I understand."

Even though they protested, Mike didn't give in. He marched the twins across the street, knowing he had to get tough. Tough. That was so far from his nature, but he had to do something with the girls. What would Laura do?

No, the real question was what would Amy do?

Chapter Three

Amy leaned her shoulder against the dining room doorway and watched her grandmother baking cookies with the twins. Worried about her relationship with the girls and her role as their teacher, Amy had made herself scarce while Grams kept an eye on them Saturday morning. She'd been cordial but stayed busy in her room, studying the textbooks and working on her lesson plans for Monday.

The twins fell into step with her grandmother without trauma. Surprised that they showed so much respect, Amy observed what Grams did, hoping to note what made the difference. She'd need to find a way to work with the twins and keep them together in the class. She wanted the opportunity to express her opinion to Mike.

She'd observed the girls' constant wavering love/ hate relationship. Competition created the problem, plus their lack of…what? What caused their need for negative attention. Mike seemed like a caring father. Maybe too caring. He tended to let them get away with a little too much. Sometimes a single parent tried to make up for the lack of the other parent by giving in to the wrong things.

Would Mike accept her help? If she said something, he could easily take it as criticism. She drew up her shoulders and released a breath. Fearing the girls might notice her, she backed away from the door and checked her watch. Mike said he should arrive home about noon—only minutes away.

Amy wandered to one of the front windows and looked toward the blue house. His wife chose the color, he'd said. Were his feelings still raw? According to Grams, it had been about three years since Mike's wife had died. Death of a spouse lay beyond her experience. She couldn't even imagine. And the poor girls. So young.

Seeing the empty driveway, she let the curtain drop, but as she did, a movement caught her eye. She looked again as Mike pulled toward the garage in the back of his yard and slid from his sedan. Hearing their murmuring voices in the kitchen, the girls were still preoccupied and that would give her a chance to slip across the road and talk with Mike before they realized he was home.

She tiptoed to the kitchen doorway, caught Grams's attention and signaled she was going out. Grams nodded, and involved with the cookies, the girls hadn't noticed. Her jacket hung in the front closet, and she slipped it on and exited through the front door. She grasped the rake she'd left on the porch and bounded down the front steps. A few additional leaves had drifted from the trees, but the yard still looked neat.

Mike had already gone inside as she crossed the road. Now that she'd made her move, she realized she might be rushing him, but her mission overrode her manners. As she approached the porch steps, the side door opened, and Mike gave her a wave. "You must be anxious to get the leaves raked."

She grinned back, admiring him in his dressy pants, cream-colored shirt and maroon tie. "I sneaked away without the twins noticing. I thought we'd have time to talk."

His face sank to concern. "Did they do something?"

She waved away her words. "No, they've been great." Now she questioned her plan to talk with him. "I just thought—"

His hand raised, stopping her apology. "Good thinking. Alone time is difficult."

The weight of discomfort lightened.

"Come in while I change." He motioned to his attire before beckoning her inside.

Although she considered going in, she had second thoughts and held up the rake. "I'll get started."

He cocked his head, shrugged and disappeared.

In a couple of minutes she'd made some progress,

but when she heard the door close, she turned and waited for Mike to join her.

Carrying a tarp along with his rake, he used his elbow to motion toward the house. "Would you rather talk first?"

Again she fought her thoughts. His earlier reaction had given her pause. "It's such a lovely day. Let's get this done."

"Okay." He grinned as he spread the tarp on the grass and dug in.

Riddled with an image of Mike making the twenty-minute drive to the school to deal with another incident, her curiosity wouldn't rest. "What do you do for a living, Mike?"

"I'm a supervisor at Oscoda Plastics a few miles south on U.S. 23."

"You're a boss?"

He gave her a sad grin. "I am there."

His plight with the girls caused her lungs to empty. His vulnerability made him not only likable but appealing. Yet beneath his grin, Mike's confidence sometimes buckled. Even though he tried to hide it, his dauntless effort failed. She was first drawn by his good looks, but today his kindness and gentle ways prickled up her arms. If she ever married one day, she would want a man like Mike—playful, sincere and with more patience than she could credit herself.

"You're quiet."

His voice jarred her thoughts and generated guilt, knowing she'd been thinking of him. "Preoccupied, I guess." She managed a grin and dug into the leaves. "I was thinking about the girls."

Mike's head lowered and he combed his fingers through his hair. "I figured you'd be concerned about having them in class."

"No, that's not it." His troubled expression made her wish she hadn't introduced the topic. "I know you feel compelled to follow the principal's suggestion to separate them, but…" She stopped raking and leaned her weight against the handle. "I suspect the girls might be worse for it. Not better."

He slowed the rake and rested his weight against it. "I had the same thought. I picture them at recess and here at home making up for the time separated." His look grew intense. "But I thought you'd be relieved having only one to deal with."

"Me?" She pressed her hand against her chest. "No, not yet anyway." She hoped to lighten the serious mood. Their conversation had drawn his lips into a straight line and stole the sparkle from his eyes. "I watched them with Grams today, and they were respectful to her and each other. I want to figure out what it is that works. I worry if they were in separate classrooms, they wouldn't learn how to get along or how to show love instead of disrespect to each other. I'd really like a chance to work with them. At least to try."

His eyes searched hers. "Are you sure?"

"Yes." She cared about them. "I don't think Mrs. Fredericks will insist on separating them. I believe she'll leave the decision up to you." A new thought fell into her mind. "If I can't handle them, maybe then she'd put pressure on you to make a decision, but not now."

His tense shoulders dropped. "If you're positive."

Amy wasn't positive she could make a difference, but she was positive she wanted to try. "Yes, I am." But Mike's concern had been for her, and although it touched her, she preferred his focus to be what was best for the girls. Rather than stir up any more tension, she let her thought fade.

He nodded as his rake hit the leaves again.

After making a pile, Mike dragged the bundle to the backyard. Three trips with the tarp made quick work of the leaves, and soon he left the tarp behind and instead dragged the leaves directly to the pile. She longed to sit and talk about a lot of things; his wife's death, the girls' reactions then and how they handled it now. Instead she gave another yank of the rake.

When the girls' squeals vibrated from behind them, she and Mike stopped raking and spun around. The twins darted toward them, but they didn't stop. Instead they barreled past, aiming for the leaf pile.

Anticipating another disaster, Amy held her breath. But this time, they dived into different sides of the mound and came up laughing. The sight trapped her in memories. The leaves drifted into the air and scattered while her heart followed. Childhood recollections drove her limbs forward, and as she sprang toward the tempting heap, Mike flew past, scooped up leaves and pitched them at her. She grabbed a handful and dashed toward him, but as she'd swung her arm to toss the colorful ammunition, she stumbled.

Mike dived forward and grabbed for her, but he missed. Both of them tumbled into the pile while the girls giggled and tossed leaves their way.

Dazed at her antics, Amy eyed Mike lying beside her, his tousled hair tangled in burnished rubble. Her heart rose to her throat.

Mike bounded to his feet and leaned down to give her his hand. She grasped his and bolted upward into his chest. Standing nose to nose, her heart tumbling to her stomach as she gazed into his eyes.

He gave her a squeeze. "Are you okay?"

His warm breath trembled across her neck. "I'm fine." But she wasn't. The closeness sent chills racing down her back. She managed a chuckle, trying to ignore the sensation as she brushed the debris from her jacket.

The girls darted from the pile, laughing at their disheveled appearance while pointing at the leaves caught in their dad's hair.

Mike shook his head, color in his cheeks alerting her of his embarrassment. "Leaves seem to bring out the child in me."

She gazed down at her jeans and jacket. "Me, too, it appears." She evaded his eyes and looked at his leaf-entangled hair. She raised her hand and pulled some out, relishing the feel of his thick mane against her fingers.

"Thanks." His flush subsided as he strode toward Holly. "Let's get you cleaned off before you drag it inside."

Amy shifted to Ivy, wanting something to distract her wavering emotions. She pulled leaves from the child's jacket and plucked them from her ponytails. When she finished, she looked at the girls, their names ringing in her mind. "Ivy and Holly." The girls turned and looked at her with question. "Where did you get those names?"

"From our mommy and daddy." Ivy grinned.

"They're Christmas names."

Holly slipped between Ivy and Amy, a leaf still caught in her hair. "Our birthday's on December 24."

Amy heart clutched. "That makes sense." She plucked the last leaf from Holly's hair, then rested her hands on their shoulders. "Did you know there's a song about holly and ivy?"

Holly shook her head. "Sing it."

Instead Mike opened his mouth and the music flowed out. "The holly and the ivy, when they are both full grown, of all the trees that are in the wood, the holly bears the crown."

His rich baritone voice enthralled her. "Mike, you have—"

"Why does holly wear a crown?" Ivy slammed her fists into her sides.

"It's the song, Ivy. I didn't make up the words." He

gestured to Amy. "And apologize to Miss Carroll. She was talking and you interrupted."

"But—"

"Apologize."

Ivy stared at her shoes. "Sorry."

Mike ignored Ivy's lack of sincerity with her apology. "What were you saying?"

"You have an astounding voice."

He flushed. "It's been years. I don't sing anymore."

"But you should."

His expression darkened for a moment before he found a grin. "Did you ever try to sing with two seven-year-olds under foot?"

Holly shook her head. "We're not under your feet."

He chuckled. "No, but you talk a lot."

Ivy gave Amy's jacket a tug. "Daddy plays the guitar, too."

Amy's senses twinged again. "Really?"

"Guilty as charged, but like singing, I…" He shrugged. "I haven't touched the guitar in a long time."

Ivy shook her head. "Sometimes at night when you think we're sleeping, we hear you."

He gazed at them for a moment. "You know it's not necessary to tell everything about me, right?" He raked his hair with his fingers

"How come you don't ever sing for us, Daddy?"

He gazed at Holly, and Amy noticed a somber look sneak to his face. "I will." He drew her closer and then reached for Ivy. "And I'll tell you later the story about the holly and ivy so you understand why the holly wears the crown, okay?"

The twins faces glowed.

Hope slid through Amy's veins. Somewhere inside the two children lived joy, and if she could find the secret to what else was going on, maybe the troublesome two could become the treasured twins.

Her task settled in her mind. She'd do everything in her power to keep those girls in her class.

Mike watched Amy cross the street, her rake like a shepherd's crook. He shuffled the girls inside wondering how he could ever explain where his heart had been for so long. Holly's blunt question about his singing had stirred up his emotions, as did Amy's compliment. *You have an astounding voice.* The words could have been Laura's. But she'd gone to heaven, and even though he didn't understand why the Lord wanted her, God saw the big picture. He didn't. She'd been the motor that revved his love of singing.

Learning the girls had heard him playing the guitar served the same purpose. And Amy, too. His heart constricted. Her caring smile hovered in his mind like a melody. Just as Amy lingered in his thoughts, music couldn't be forgotten either. It revived his spirit. Amy's presence had done the same.

"You said you'd tell us, Daddy."

Ivy's voice broke his train of thought. He gazed at her sweet face and knelt on the kitchen floor, drawing the two girls into his arms. "Your mom always nagged me about singing and playing the guitar. Because she's not here, I guess it left my thoughts."

"Did Mom leave your thoughts?"

Holly's troubled expression caused him dismay. "Never. I promised God to love her always, and I will, but that doesn't mean I don't have lots of love to share."

"With us?"

"With you." He paused, trying to word his next statement. "And maybe someday, I might meet someone who could be in our lives, too."

"Like Amy?"

Ivy's question tripped through his veins.

"Someone like that. Someone who's nice and likes both of you."

Holly's eyes narrowed. "Maybe Miss Carroll doesn't like us?"

"I think she does, don't you, Daddy?"

Ivy's response gave his answer. "Yes. She wants to keep you together in class."

"She does?" Their eyes widened.

"Unless you cause her trouble, and then she won't want to deal with your antics."

Holly scrutinized him again. "What's antics?"

"Your behavior. You know, how you act up sometimes."

Ivy gave her a poke. "Like choking me."

"Or tripping me."

"You both do things to each other. I know you still

love each other, but sometimes it doesn't seem that way to other people." He drew the girls in closer. "Remember what you said the other day? You told me you were all you had?"

They nodded. "You need to let people see how much you mean to each other. Hurting each other and misbehaving isn't the way to do that."

Ivy straightened. "It's Holly's fault."

He tightened his grip before a new argument began. "It's both of your faults. And that's enough about it. I don't want to hear another word."

They quieted, but he suspected each girl was working on a comeback. "Now, I'll hand you a rake, Ivy, and I'll get another one for Holly. Because you two were the first ones to spread the leaf pile, it's your job to clean it up."

"But—"

Without listening further, he handed Ivy the rake and headed to his shed. He didn't turn around until he arrived at the storage unit and pulled out the rake. When he looked back, Holly had gotten on her knees and was dragging the leaves into the pile with her arms. Elation rippled over him. He loved seeing the girls work or play without arguing. Diving into the leaves had brightened everyone's spirits. He hadn't felt like that in years.

"Here you go." He handed Holly the rake, then relieved Ivy of hers.

She didn't argue but followed Holly's example and

tossed the leaves back into the pile. "Can we burn them?" She gazed up at him with a smile in her eyes.

"Maybe later tonight."

"Can we make s'mores?"

He chuckled. "Not over the leaves, Holly, but maybe we can make some inside."

Ivy licked her lips. "Can we invite Miss Carroll? I bet she likes s'mores."

His chest tightened. "Not tonight." He looked across the yard to Ellie's house, wanting to include Amy in everything but cautioning himself to move slowly. To be certain. To understand his feelings and the ramifications.

He started preparing their dinner, but his mind dwelt on Amy and the delicate situation. He really liked her, but it unsettled him. Having feelings for a woman other than Laura dragged him back to his dating days. But when he'd met Laura, his interest for any other woman had faded.

After all those years, he wasn't sure he could handle another relationship without feeling guilty. And what about the girls? Would familiarity with Amy make them too forward in school? That would never work. He pondered the idea for a moment before making a decisive decision.

He had to cool it.

Chapter Four

Amy erased the blackboard and eyed the clock. She'd noticed buses arriving, and soon the halls would be quiet. Her first day on the job had been exciting. After her layoff in Chicago, teaching again so soon had seemed a hopeless dream. Yet here she was. She settled into her desk chair and breathed in the scent of chalk, floor polish and the beguiling scent of textbooks. She grinned.

When she gazed at the empty rows of chairs, she had pictured the twins sitting close together, eyeing each other while temptation crooked a finger, but they'd been perfect. But Amy faced reality. Thinking the girls would remain perfect was definitely a lofty goal.

Grams had a way with Ivy and Holly, but her only recommendation to Amy was to love them. She heaved a sigh. Mike loved them, but that didn't work for him.

The sound of quiet echoed in the halls—the hum of fluorescent lighting and the yawn of a distant door. She eyed the stack of papers on her desk and drew them toward her, wanting to grade them by tomorrow. She'd asked the children to write a paragraph on how they would spend Thanksgiving. Hearing how they would celebrate the holiday could give her an inside look at their families and their traditions. Coming into the semester late meant she needed a quick way to gain insight into her students' lives.

"Miss Carroll."

Amy jerked at the familiar voice. She eyed her watch. "Ivy, shouldn't you be on the bus?"

Holly slipped past her sister into the room. "We missed it."

"Missed it?" She studied both of the girls. "How did you do that?"

"Ivy went to the bathroom."

Ivy strutted forward shaking her head at Holly. "Uh-uh. You went and I followed."

Now what? She studied their faces, aware of what they expected. "Maybe there's another bus going your way. Let's go down to the office."

"There's not." The too-familiar determined look settled on Holly's face.

She ignored her. "We need to check." She rose and strode through the doorway, hearing two sets of footsteps behind her.

When she entered the front office, Sue Murphy, the secretary, arched an eyebrow. "What are you two doing here?"

"We missed the bus, because Ivy—"

"Uh-uh. It was Holly's fault."

"The last bus left. I'll have to notify your driver so he doesn't worry and then call your dad." Sue braced her hands against the counter. "He's not going to be very happy."

Ivy bustled closer. "You don't have to call our dad."

Holly shouldered her sister out of the way. "We can ride home with Miss Carroll. She lives on our street."

The woman peered at her. "Are you okay with this?"

She bit her lip. This was what she feared—the girls becoming too familiar and taking advantage. "Would you check with their father first?"

"Certainly."

Amy studied the twins' eager faces, and thought of Mike being dragged home from work again. The girls often went to her grandmother's anyway or a sitter came in until Mike arrived home. She evaded the twins' pleading looks and focused on Sue's telephone conversation. Watching the secretary's head nod gave Amy her answer. Mike had agreed.

When the girls learned he'd agreed she drive them home, their faces brightened. Amy's didn't. Her plan to work on tomorrow's lessons at her school desk ended with the new development.

She strode back to her room, slipped on her coat, gathered the homework papers and her planning book and then herded the twins outside. Once in the car, she faced them in the backseat. "You can't do this everyday, girls. Some days I need to stay here and work. I'm sure you'd rather be home with a sitter or with Gramma Ellic."

Restrained by the seat belts, Holly leaned as close as she could. "We could help you."

Ivy nodded in agreement.

Amy started the car. "Not when I'm planning lessons and correcting papers," Amy said.

"But we could—"

"That won't work." Amy used her teacher's voice. "Next time I'll have Mrs. Murphy call your dad to pick you up."

Ivy's face sank. "He'll be mad."

"Right." She backed her car out of the spot.

The fifteen-minute ride home remained restrained except for a few comments the girls made to each other. Amy wished she could hear because she suspected they were plotting. When she pulled into the driveway, the two tumbled out and darted to Grams's side door. She sat a moment, determined to come up with a way to discourage their ploy from happening again.

When she stepped inside the house, voices came from the kitchen, and as she passed the door, she gave her grandmother a wave and went directly to her room. She tossed her coat on a chair and slipped off her shoes, settling her feet into her fuzzy slippers. The weather had turned cold since they'd raked on Saturday. That evening, she'd watched Mike burning leaves, and she'd longed to wander over but forced herself to stay away. And although she considered her decision wise, especially after the girls' shenanigans today, part of her hoped that Mike would invite her over to sit with him as he monitored the fire.

She shook her head. The last thing she wanted was to jeopardize her teaching position or allow her heart to tangle around a widowed man and his daughters. That could easily lead to heartbreak. Plus she was certain she wouldn't live forever in a small town. Chicago's excitement lured her back.

Amy pulled on a sweatshirt before settling on the bed. She leaned forward and grasped the stack of papers she'd brought home. She read the first child's paragraph relating how the family watched football on TV and he listed the Thanksgiving dinner menu. While she made a note of spelling errors, her curiosity led her to search for the twins' papers in the pile.

Skimming Holly's paper, her heart sank.

"Daddy takes us to Mama's Country Kitchin for diner on Thanksgiving. Daddy says a prayer, and we say what we give thanks for. Then we have turkey, mashed potatoes and gravy. Then we have punkin pie."

A restaurant for Thanksgiving? Her throat tightened as her eyes flashed across Ivy's paper. Better spelling didn't brighten the message.

"On Thanksgiving, Daddy takes us out to eat, but what I wish is that we could eat at home. We did when our mom was alive. Now Thanksgiving is different. But I am happy that I have a dad who loves me. We say thank you for all good things before we eat."

Amy brushed tears from her eyes, trying to hold back a flood of them. Her own childhood memories of Thanksgivings and Christmases came to mind, when she, too, ached for a mother in her life. As she grew older, she'd tried to concentrate on the positives in her life, but the old haunting ache remained just as it had surfaced today.

Determination pried its way into her mind. Even though she'd been set on keeping her distance with the twins, how could she when Mike and the girls ate Thanksgiving dinner in a restaurant?

Before Amy had moved to Harrisville, her grandmother often spent holiday meals with church friends, but Grams had announced this year they would celebrate at home. The glint in her grandmother's eye made Amy realize Grams had been lonely for family. So had she for all the years living in Illinois, first with only her father and later alone in an apartment.

The papers slipped from her fingers, and Amy leaned back against the pillow, fighting heavy eyes and a heavy heart. She lowered her lids for a moment, thinking a couple minutes' rest might refresh her after the first day of her new job.

The scent of cookies drifted into her room, and Amy bolted upward, eyeing the clock. She'd slept for over an hour. Voices penetrated her bedroom door, including a man's voice.

Mike.

She swung her legs over the edge of the mattress and sat up. As she did, some of the papers fluttered to the floor. She rose, gathered them and tossed them on the bed. Then eyeing herself in the vanity mirror, she grabbed a comb and ran her hands through the tangles, then headed for the door.

As her hand hit the knob, a surge of apprehension swept over her as she considered talking with Grams about Mike and the girls. No one should eat Thanksgiving dinner in a restaurant. Yet she pushed the idea out of her mind for the moment and opened the door. She needed distance, or she'd face the ramifications at school.

"There you are." Grams gave her a welcoming smile.

"I smelled the cookies." She looked at Mike. "I didn't realize so much time had passed."

A crooked smile lit his face. "I like your footwear."

She looked down at her fuzzy slippers, and her cheeks heated.

Grams gave a chuckle as she ran a spatula beneath a freshly baked cookie and set it on a plate. "What were you doing in there so long? I figured you'd be out here after the first batch of cookies."

The question slid down her spine. "I brought home work from school. You know, papers I need to correct."

Mike grinned. "First day on the job and you're already correcting papers?"

"It's a teacher's life." She realized the twins flanked him, their eyes wide and questioning. She'd already decided not to make an issue out of their little ploy.

"Thanks for driving the girls home." His words rang with discouragement.

A lump formed in her throat. "You're welcome."

He placed a hand on the top of each girl's head. "I told them no more missing the bus. I don't expect you to chauffeur them home from school because they were dallying."

"But Daddy, I told you—"

Mike held up a finger, and the girls' opened mouths closed.

"I've already explained I can't give them a ride all the time." She pressed her lips together to stop speaking. She knew in her heart, if he needed her to, she would.

"More cookies, girls?" Grams extended the plate.

But Mike held up his hand. "I think we've all had enough. One more, and we won't want dinner."

His comment drew Amy's attention to the girls. They had a trace of a white mustache and a few crumbs on their cheeks and lips.

Mike brushed crumbs from the front of his shirt. "We need to get home, but thanks so much for the treat, Ellie, and for watching the girls."

"It's always a pleasure, and don't forget my invitation." Her grandmother's face glowed.

Invitation? Amy's gaze shifted from her grandmother to Mike.

"Your home cooking beats Mama's Country Kitchen any day of the week. Thanks for your generous offer."

The girls bounced on their toes, their faces filled with glee. "Can we, Daddy? Really?"

He drew closer to Holly. "If you learn to behave in school."

"I behave."

"They were excellent in class today." Amy gave him a tender smile.

"Good." Mike wrapped an arm around each girl. "If they can keep that up until Thanksgiving, I'll be pleased to accept your invitation."

Amy's pulse kicked up a notch. What could she do? Grams had asked, and she would deal with it. While a warmth spread through her chest, beneath her buoyant thoughts, a caution sign blinked.

Mike watched the snowflakes drift into piles against the house next door. Winter had made its appearance in time for Thanksgiving. He'd held his breath since he'd made his proclamation about the Thanksgiving invitation, but Holly and Ivy had made it through the rest of the week without incident. At least, he hadn't been notified. He avoided putting Amy on the spot by calling her to check, even though he'd been tempted. In his heart he knew his girls' behavior would have only been a cover for his real motive. He liked Amy—a lot.

And he marveled at how much Ivy and Holly liked her. Amy seemed innovative with their lessons. Each day after school when he arrived home from work, they gave him details of stories they read, paragraphs they'd written, games they'd played with their math problems, and how they were making a bulletin board of all their drawings of different kinds of animals they were studying. Their enthusiasm bolstered his spirit.

He rose from the kitchen table and strode to the hallway, wondering if they were awake. "Did you see the snow?"

A rustle sounded in their bedrooms, and he guessed they'd just crawled out of bed. He glanced at his watch. Nine. He could have waited. His peaceful Saturday morning always ended once the girls roused from their rooms.

Holly popped her head out the door. "Can we make a snowman?"

"First I thought we'd go out to breakfast."

"Breakfast!" Ivy appeared in pants and her pajama top. "Can we?"

"Get ready."

Looking forward to eating out, the twins made

quick work of getting dressed, and they were all on their way in minutes. Mike drove down Main Street and pulled into the Flour Garden. Inside, he greeted the owner, Manny, as he passed through the small store filled with the scent of fresh ground coffee, then past the bakery counter, Mike found a booth along the wall. He looked out the window and watched flakes setting on the large evergreen across the street. Tomorrow it would be decorated for Christmas, and the town would gather for the tree-lighting. The event lured people from their cozy homes to listen to the music and enjoy the cookies and hot chocolate as they sang carols and joined in the festivities.

Mike pulled his gaze from the snow-covered knoll and chatted with a couple of his neighbors before he perused the menu. When Jill appeared to take their order, she offered her usual smile and patiently waited while the girls decided on their choices. Mike wondered why they took so long. They usually ordered pancakes. Today was no different.

He barely downed his first cup of coffee when the food arrived, and the twins became silent as they delved into the pancakes and drank their juice. Before Mike had time to make a dent in his meal, Holly's voice jerked his attention.

"I'm finished."

Mike lowered his coffee cup and eyed her plate. She had indeed gobbled down her food. "You'll get sick eating so fast."

"But I'm anxious to make a snowman."

Ivy took a bite of her pancake and rolled her eyes. "You eat like a pig."

Holly spun around and grabbed one of Ivy's pony-tails and gave it a jerk. "I do not."

Mike held up his hand. "We don't talk to people like that."

Ivy started to roll her eyes again before she caught herself. "Sorry."

He gave Holly a pointed look. "And you don't pull people's hair." His fun morning vanished like a snowman in the sun. He signaled the waitress for the bill. After she slipped the tab on the table, he snatched it off, put on his coat and trudged to the cashier.

The girls squabbled behind him, each blaming the other while he tried to close his ears. One moment he rallied, and the next moment his hopes sagged. Discouraged, he trudged outside.

The sun had slipped from behind the clouds, sending prisms of light across the fluffy flakes. Mike wished his spirit shone as bright as the landscape.

"Daddy?"

He gave Ivy a fleeting glance. "What?"

"I'm sorry. I won't call Holly a pig ever again."

He didn't know if he should laugh or groan. "Thank you."

"And I won't choke Ivy anymore. I promise," Holly mumbled.

When he looked at their hangdog expressions, his anger faded. "Why do you do this? Every time

I think we'll have a nice day, you ruin it with your horrible behavior."

Tears brimmed Ivy's eyes, and even Holly looked crestfallen. He knelt on the ground, the snow wetting his knees. "I don't enjoy being upset with you. Do you know that?" He slipped his arms around them. "But you can't keep acting like this. Instead of being proud of you both, you disappoint me, and…" His voice locked in his throat.

Instead of responding, Ivy threw her arms around his neck and kissed his cheek. "We'll be good, Daddy."

Holly only nodded.

He gazed at Ivy, wanting to remind her that she'd said the same thing before.

"I suppose we can't make a snowman now."

He rose without answering and unlocked the car's door. After the girls slipped in, he pulled away from the restaurant still weighing his thoughts.

As he approached Third Street, he turned right. Instead of home, he headed for Harrisville State Park. For once he was doing something for himself and in the process, delayed the snowman issue. He loved seeing the untrodden snow along the breadth of the shore and the white snowfall weighing the evergreen boughs.

The girls' muttering let him know they were curious, but neither asked where they were going. He veered into the parking area to the girls' outcries of pleasure, and as he rolled into a spot, his heart skipped when he saw the familiar dark orange hatchback.

"Miss Carroll's here."

Their voices sailed to him in unison. He heard the snap of their seat belts, and their door opened as a damp chill whisked into the car. He turned off the motor and stepped outside, both curious and anxious. He'd longed to see Amy again, but he hadn't found a good excuse. Now he didn't need one.

The twins shot ahead of him, slipping and skittering past the pavilion filled with snow-covered picnic tables. When Amy heard them, she swung around, surprise on her face, and when her eyes met his, she smiled.

But the expression appeared strained, and he faltered. "Sorry to disturb you." His breath billowed in a white mist.

"The park's public." Her smile settled to a grin. "I haven't been to the park since I moved here, and I knew it would look lovely in the snow."

He agreed. "We're heading home from breakfast."

She gazed at him in silence.

He peered at his boots ankle deep in snow and tucked his hands into his pockets. He'd forgotten his gloves in the car. Tongue-tied, he searched for something to say. Then he noticed she carried a camera. "Taking photos?"

She held it up and nodded. "I want to send a few to some friends in Chicago. They don't see pristine settings like this very often."

"Do you live in downtown Chicago?" Mike knew little about her except what Ellie happened to mention.

"I did until I lost my job."

Now he remembered Ellie had told him about her job. "I suppose it was difficult to leave a big city for such a small town."

A one shoulder shrug was her response.

"And leaving your friends."

"In a way. But I wanted to spend time with Grams, so it seemed a good time to make the change. It is different here."

Before he could learn more, she walked away, stopping to snap a few photos.

When the girls noticed her camera, they waved. "Take a picture of us."

Holly dashed for one slide and Ivy for the other. They climbed the snow-covered stairs and plopped onto the wet top before he could stop them. Feeling the cold through his boots, he could only imagine the chill the girls felt sitting on the icy metal. Amy stood between the two slides and snapped one photo then another as they slid to the ground. Their laughter echoed in the quiet. If only his troubles could be whisked away by laughter.

Ivy skipped to Amy followed by Holly, and she let them look at the digital photographs. As he approached, Holly waved him closer. "Look at our picture."

He tilted the camera and admired the photographs she'd taken. "Very nice."

"In the city, we have white snow for a few minutes before it turns to gray slush. I want my friends to see how pretty the snow is here."

Her reference to friends caused him to twinge. Maybe a man waited for her in Chicago.

Ivy nestled in between them. "We're going to make a snowman when we get home." She tilted her head, giving him a plea-filled look. "Aren't we, Daddy?"

Holly eyed him, too, and his frustration waned. "That was our plan."

To Mike's discomfort, Ivy pressed the situation. "Want to come over and help?"

Amy rocked from one foot to the other. "I'm not sure your dad needs help."

Holly jerked his jacket. "You do, don't you?"

He swallowed. "A really good snowman takes a lot of talented people."

"Then you can help us, Miss Carroll. You're talented."

The uneasy feeling he'd felt earlier vanished when he heard Amy's chuckle. "How can I say no to such a compliment?"

Her smile thawed his icy thoughts while he basked in summery hopes.

Chapter Five

"I can't believe they're still outside." Mike stood at the window gazing into his front yard watching the twins build a snowdog for the snowman. "They're doing a good job."

Amy rose and joined him at the front window. "Very creative, I'd say."

Even though his eyes were on the girls, his senses were alive with Amy's closeness. So near, his gaze swept across her flawless skin, her cheeks still highlighted by the crisp cold. Her pink lips smiled, soft and full.

His lungs constricted, forcing his thoughts to cool it. He closed his eyes and sucked in air. "How about some of that hot chocolate the girls talked about?"

"Sounds good." Her eyes flickered with uncertainty, yet her gaze clung to his, and he knew they were trying to read each other but both seemed unsuccessful.

He strode to the kitchen, needing to do something to keep his mind busy. He turned on the burner beneath the teakettle and opened the cabinet to pull out the mugs.

In seconds, she followed. "Can I help?"

"This is easy." He lifted the hot chocolate mix and pointed to the label. "Just add hot water." But then he pointed to an upper cabinet. "You can find the marshmallows, if you want. They're up there somewhere."

She found them quicker than he might have and set them on the counter.

"Please, have a seat." He motioned toward the kitchen table, needing the distance. "The water will take a couple of minutes."

Amy shifted the chair and sat, watching him.

Silence buzzed in his ears, and he searched through his thoughts for conversation. Seeing her in his kitchen, so fresh and appealing, his tongue had tied again.

"Mike, does it bother you to talk about your wife?"

"Laura?" The question whisked through his mind. "No, not anymore." He pulled out the chair adjacent to hers and slipped into it. "Why?"

She shrugged, a gentle expression swept over her face. "I think about the girls growing up without a mom, and I..."

"You feel bad for them."

Her eyes searched his face. "No, but I understand. I've been there."

Her comment jarred him. "Really?"

"I lost my mom when I was four."

The sadness in her eyes flooded over him. "I'm so sorry, Amy. I didn't know."

She shrugged again. "Things happen, and we make it through. But I remember longing to be like the other kids and having a mom as they did. My father tried so hard to be both mother and father to me, but…"

A chill prickled down Mike's arms. He wanted to fill in the blank yet he had no words.

She finally lifted her head and her eyes captured his. "My dad tried too hard, and when he felt helpless, he gave up. I had no idea what to do, and I felt responsible. I was six or seven when I took on the burden of my dad's failure and his unhappiness."

Failure. Unhappiness. Six or seven. The words spilled over him, and he suffocated with the weight. Her comment buried him in thought until he managed to take a full breath. "Is that what I'm doing?"

"Maybe." Her eyes searched his. "I know you're trying to be a good dad, but a father is all you can be. You can't be a mother. Not really." She reached across the space and rested her hand on his. "But that's okay because you can be the greatest dad. That's important."

Overwhelmed, he struggled to grasp her words. "But how?"

"Lose the guilt."

Memories flooded him—his talks with Laura

about having a baby and her desire to wait. Why hadn't he listened to her? He couldn't deny his guilt. The talks with Laura were one-sided. He'd bugged her, wanting to be a dad. Wanting to be a family.

Tenderness etched Amy's face and rent him in two.

"I do feel guilty sometimes, and I know I've failed them."

"Oh, Mike." Her hand squeezed his. "You're a great dad. Look at today, with the snowman and out to breakfast. You dote on them, but that's part of the problem. You can love them, but they need firm directions without you giving in to their pleading. You're gentle, but you need to be tough. I know that's difficult for you."

He gave her a slow nod, understanding fully what she'd just said. "I've been realizing lately that I let them bully me. I give in to their demands. Holly barks, and I jump."

"She's a strong character, but Ivy has her way, too. She's the clinger, just like her name. She beguiles you with her sweet, pleading face."

He lowered his head with a chuckle. "You're certainly observant."

She grinned. "Teachers take a lot of psychology classes. Too bad they can't apply it to their own problems, but it helps to understand why people behave as they do."

That's what Amy had been doing all along. Using her psychology training. He was the parent of two troublesome twins. Naturally she wanted to help the girls, and in the process make her teaching easier. Even though he appreciated her motivation for friendship, the reality left an emptiness in his chest.

Amy eyed him, a scowl edging out her tender look. "Mike, I've hurt your feelings. I'm so sorry."

"No." He slipped his hand from beneath hers and straightened. "You've helped me face reality."

Her scowl deepened.

"I mean you gave me good advice. You're right. I'm spoiling the girls. Real life doesn't work that way. Not everything goes the way we want it to." The words tore into him, and in the distance, he heard the whistling of the teakettle. He rose. But the sweetness had vanished.

When he looked at her, Amy hadn't moved, but her face registered awareness that their mood had changed. Her expression twisted his heart.

She rose. "Maybe I should go."

Their conversation skittered to a halt. Maybe he'd misread her comments. Trying to decipher Amy had troubled him from the start. "Please. Stay. Let's have the hot chocolate."

Her expression didn't change, but she sank back into the chair.

He stirred water into the chocolate mix and popped marshmallows into the mug. "Hot chocolate cures what ails you."

He set the mug in front of her and made a cup for himself. When he returned to the chair, he knew he had to change the subject. "Do you miss Chicago?"

Despite the hot chocolate, cold anticipation washed over him.

"I love the city." Her gaze drifted toward the back window looking out into the snowy woods behind the house.

He held his breath.

"But I spent lots of time in Harrisville when Dad and I came to visit Grams. I consider this my second home."

His own past came to mind. "I grew up in Cincinnati, but I've learned to love the quiet of small town living. It's like one big family in a way."

"It is." Yet her eyes said something else. "Not sure I could live in a small town permanently. I worry I'd be bored."

The response he'd anticipated sent an icy chill up his spine. If he really wanted to cool his feelings, he would want her to go to Chicago. But he didn't.

Her gaze caught his. "But right now, unless a job offer calls me back, I'm here."

He tried again. "Anyone special you've left behind?"

She shifted her gaze from his eyes, a thoughtful look spreading over her face. "No one special. Coworkers and people I've gotten to know in my apartment building. But friends can be found everywhere." She locked eyes with him.

"Everywhere." Did she refer to the twins or did she like him, too? Caution told him to change the subject.

Yet he opened his mouth, a feeler comment fell out. "I've enjoyed meeting you, Amy."

She searched his face as she lifted her cup and took a sip. "I have to admit I've met some nice people here." She gave him a full smile.

The tension between them slipped away with her smile. His relationship with Amy confused him, and he wasn't sure what he expected, but being a dad didn't negate being a man. Right now he would enjoy her friendship.

Amy sipped her hot chocolate, watching him.

"Have you been in Harrisville for the Christmas tree-lighting celebration?"

"You mean the one they decorate on U.S. 23?"

"Right. It's a big occasion."

"I've never been here for that." Her eyes lowered to the hot chocolate. "When is it?"

"Tomorrow. It's always the Sunday before Thanksgiving."

She wrapped her fingers around the mug. "Are you and the girls going?"

His lungs emptied as he tried to keep his mind thinking friendship. "I wouldn't miss it. Carols, hot chocolate and cookies, music. The whole community shows up."

"Sounds nice."

Mike studied her a moment. "Would you like to join us?"

"Tomorrow?"

"The Goodfellows light the tree at dusk. About

five o'clock, but the caroling and hot chocolate start at four. You'd be welcome to come with us." His pulse skipped. "I know the girls would love it." And if he was completely honest, so would he.

Her head inched upward. "I'd love to."

"Daddy, come look." The door banged into the wall as the twins called out in unison.

Mike jerked upward, his mind still reeling with her eager acceptance. "I guess I'd better look."

Amy carried the mug and strode beside him into the living room.

A sense of wholeness rolled through him for the first time in three years.

"Joy to the world, the Lord is come. Let Earth receive her King." Mike's rich voice soared through the air to the strum of a guitar and took Amy's spirit with it. She pulled her scarf higher up around her neck, feeling the melody wrap around her soul. Today not only the hot chocolate but also the music warmed her heart.

Ivy and Holly had shifted closer to the huge evergreen tree decorated with colorful lights soon to be turned on, but even from a distance, Amy witnessed the cookie crumbs on the front of the girls' jackets. She grinned, gazing at their wide eyes as if they'd never attended a tree-lighting ceremony before, though Mike said they came every year.

So many people had stopped to greet Mike, and he'd introduced her to them. She'd met Deidre Gray, owner of Maggie's On Main, a gift shop she'd passed often but hadn't stopped in yet. She looked forward to shopping there, wanting to purchase something special for Grams as a Christmas gift.

Everyone seemed to like Mike. He greeted them with a bright smile, trying to cover the discouragement she sometimes saw in his eyes. Mike had said more than once that he'd overcome the grief of his wife's death, but something clung to the memory no matter how many years it had been. She should understand. After twenty-five years, her mother's disappearance still remained an open wound.

When Mike touched her arm, Amy jerked. "It's almost time." He pointed to the tree.

She craned her neck around the heads of adults standing in front of her and saw the girls bouncing, gigantic smiles on their faces, their blue eyes round as the moon. She shot Mike a grin. The guitar began to strum again, and she longed to see Mike there leading the music. The crowd joined in singing the familiar carol, "We Wish You a Merry Christmas," as the lights sparked into a colorful display on the tree.

Even though uneasy with her singing ability, she sang with the others. "We wish you a merry Christmas, we wish you a merry Christmas and a happy New Year."

Mike's baritone voice bolstered her confidence. He slipped his arm behind her back and gave her a hug. Touched by his enthusiasm, she leaned into his warmth and the comfort of his closeness. He smiled at her, and caught up in the excitement, she beamed back. The music, the lighted tree, the twins' smiles, the warmth of Christmas wrapped her in a holiday package.

"Mike, thanks for inviting me. This was wonderful."

He drew her even closer. "This is just the beginning. Wait until we have Christmas in the Village."

"You mean Christmas Eve?"

"That, too, but I'm talking about December third. Everything happens the first Saturday in December."

Amy was confused. "What do you mean everything happens?"

"Craft bazaars, the annual cookie walk and bake sale, Santa at the library with activities for children and the stores offer shopping specials." He gave her a teasing poke. "We can even go on a hayride, and then you can warm up with cider at the Harrisville Arts Council."

"That does sound like everything." Her head reeled with the list of activities.

"Put it on your calendar."

Her calendar. Mike had been a major part of her calendar, and the whole idea threw her off balance. Her determination to remain uninvolved had turned to ash. Amy managed a grin, but caught in confusion she evaded his gaze. He seemed to see too much in her eyes. Right now she didn't understand herself, so she didn't want him making wild guesses.

As some of the crowd moved on toward the hot chocolate and some toward their cars, she waited while Mike rounded up the girls. Although the joy of Christmas filled her, beneath it, impending concerns edged into her thoughts. Falling for this man created too many problems. The girls were her students, she loved Chicago and belonged there, her father's deep sadness and too many failed marriages among people she knew. The relationship was a puzzle with pieces that didn't fit. She either needed to get a grip now or throw herself into the fray while she prayed the Lord was guiding her path. A God she hadn't talked to in a long time.

Chapter Six

The scent of roasted turkey drifted from the oven. Amy licked her fingers, tasting the tangy cranberry-and-orange relish she'd made for their dinner. She'd also contributed the pumpkin pies with Grams's guidance. Having no mom to teach her to cook, her skills had been hit or miss, but not when Grams was around. Her grandmother didn't accept mediocrity when it came to cooking, especially with Thanksgiving dinner. Amy's heart soared when the pies came from the oven yesterday afternoon, looking and smelling perfect, just like Grams's.

Lifting the bowl of cranberry sauce, she turned and caught her grandmother gazing at her. "Are you checking on me?" She grinned.

No smile slipped to her Grams's lips. "I'm thinking."

Amy's legs turned to mush. When Grams had

something on her mind, she didn't hide her feelings. "What's wrong?"

Her grandmother clasped the back of a chair and pulled it out, then sank to the seat and gave Amy a look.

She didn't have to ask. Grams wanted to talk about her not going to church. Amy slipped onto the chair, waiting for her grandmother's sage wisdom about what Jesus expected. She'd meant to go because she knew church was important to her grandmother, but she had formed a bad habit, following her father's lead. He'd withdrawn from everything after her mother vanished.

"You know I love you, Amy."

"I love you, too, Grams."

"I've been thinking about this for a long time, and I—" She shook her head. "I just can't keep quiet any longer."

Amy searched her grandmother's face.

"How long are you planning to stay in Harrisville?"

Amy's stomach twisted in knots. "I—I agreed to finish out the school year, Grams. That's in June. Have I done something?" Panic ripped through her. "Do you want me to find another place to stay?"

"No, honey. What would give you that idea?" Sadness filled her eyes. "I love having you here, but I'm concerned."

"Concerned?"

"About Mike and the girls. You're spending an awful lot of time with them."

Amy's head spun and she broke eye contact. Grams had been the one to invite them to dinner. But it was more than that. Mike had stepped into her life and filled it. "Does that bother you?"

"I care about them, Amy, just like I care about you. I've watched them finally begin to heal from Laura's death, and I worry that…that Mike's feelings have grown for you. And those little girls, too—and one of these days—"

"I'll walk away and leave them." The words flew from her mouth before she could stop thinking.

"Yes." Her grandmother's face sank as her eyes lowered to her apron. "It would break their hearts."

Amy held her breath. Nothing could remedy the reality that one day she might go back. Part of her cherished Harrisville, but Chicago lingered in her mind. Its life and vigor. Fun and education at her fingertips. The skyscrapers soaring toward heaven. Cars like bugs skittering along the streets to escape red lights and traffic jams. The city was alive.

Amy faced her grandmother. "I've thought about that, too. I'm torn. I care about the twins, and Mike is the greatest. If I ever fell in love, it could easily be with a man like him."

Grams smoothed the wrinkle in her apron. "Why *haven't* you ever fallen in love?"

A weight stooped her shoulders. "I—" Amy sought the words, something that would make sense to her grandmother without hurting her. "You didn't see Dad after Mom left, Grams. He lost his spirit. He sank into a pit and never came out, even though he tried to put on a good front when he came here to visit."

"I'm not blind, Amy. I could see that, but what does that have to do with you, other than feeling bad for your dad?"

"It's not just his marriage. I've worked with people whose marriages failed. They either sink into an abyss or they dive off the high board into an empty pool. They get silly, run around and get involved in empty relationships to hide their pain. If I never fall in love, then I don't have to deal with that. I can hang on to my heart without having it ripped out of my chest."

"Oh, Amy." Her grandmother lowered her head, rocking it back and forth as if what she'd said had devastated her.

"Grams, I—"

"I understand what you're saying, but that's not how the heart works. When you close your heart, you close it to every relationship because you're not willing to take a chance at being vulnerable. You can't live a full life like that."

"My life is full. I have friends and I had a good job until—"

"Friends are important. A job gives security, but Amy, what makes life full or complete? Can a job or friends do that?"

"I thought so." Her heart sank when she uttered the words. She knew better. Many times an emptiness worked its way through her.

"I know your dad turned his back on the Lord. It's not how we raised him, but he lost his way, and my only hope is now that he's learned that your mom has passed, he'll rebuild his life again."

"He's dating a nice lady, Grams. That's what he tells me. He's spending Thanksgiving with her family today. I'm happy for him."

The tension in her face softened. "So am I. Your dad remained married to your mother despite what she'd done, running off and living with a man all those years. It's not my job to judge. I leave that to the Lord, but I know it hurt you both. Deeply. If I could have made it better I would have, but I never thought it would end your dreams of having a family one day. Never. You love children. The Lord gives us talents. Yours is working with children. Mine's cooking." A grin eased her face. "And loving your grandpa, and I didn't do too badly raising our son."

"He's a good person, Grams. He just became lost." Memories flooded her. "Dad tried so hard, but he couldn't connect with me. When Mom left, I— I don't know. I guess I closed down, too, and later I felt guilty, knowing I had turned my back on Dad. I blame myself for his unhappiness."

A gasp escaped Grams. "No! You were always his joy."

"But I didn't know how to make him better."

"You were four years old. How could you be the cause or the solution?" Her tongue made tsking sounds as she shook her head. "I wish we'd talked about this years ago."

Amy grabbed her grandmother's hand. "So do I." Today she'd exposed her feelings for the first time. They'd bored into her mind, turning and twisting while she tried to make sense of them.

She lifted her grandmother's hand and pressed her lips to her crepey skin. "I'll be open and honest with Mike before anything happens. I won't make promises I can't keep."

Her grandmother gave her hand a squeeze. "You're a good girl, Amy. I just couldn't hold all this in when—"

The doorbell jarred their conversation.

Amy rose. "I'll let them in, Grams. Don't worry, please."

Even though her grandmother nodded, Amy wasn't fooled. Grams was worried, but then so was she.

Mike pushed away his empty dessert plate and grinned at Ellie, still wrapped in a big apron. "These pies were excellent. Your best."

She chuckled and gave a nod toward Amy. "You'll have to thank my granddaughter. Amy made the pies."

Amy's cheeks turned rosy. "But I used Grams's recipe. I'm not much of a cook."

"If these pies are any evidence, I think you're

wrong." Mike tossed off the comment casually, but he was seriously worried. Amy had been quiet today. Withdrawn even, and he didn't understand why. The last time they were together at the tree-lighting, she'd been sweet, thanking him for inviting her. They'd even made plans for Saturday's Christmas in the Village.

"Holly. Ivy." Grams's voice cut into his thoughts. "I have a surprise for you."

"A surprise." Holly slipped from the chair.

Grams grinned. "A gift, but you'll have to help me get it ready."

Ivy tilted her head. "But it's not even Christmas yet."

"This present helps you get ready for Christmas." She beckoned them to follow.

Mike watched them go, leaving him alone with Amy. An uneasy feeling wiggled along his limbs. She confused him.

"Would you like more coffee?"

He pushed aside his uneasy feelings. "Sure. Thanks."

Amy strode from the room while he drew in a lengthy breath. When she came through the doorway, she headed toward him with the coffee carafe, filled his cup and then her own before settling back into her chair.

"Grams made the girls an Advent calendar."

"Ellie's always thoughtful." From her expression, he detected she saw it as a comparison. "That's where you've learned your kindness, I'm sure." She flinched, and he wished he'd kept his mouth closed.

"No one has the heart that Grams has. She's one of a kind."

He wanted to argue the point, but he sensed it would be purposeless. Quiet settled over them as he scrambled for conversation. "Did you send the photos of the snow to your friends in Chicago?"

"I did. A few wrote back how much they envied me." She looked as though she had more to say. He waited, but she remained quiet.

"I suppose some of them do. I suspect you won't agree, but I think you fit in here, and we both know it makes your grandmother happy."

She didn't respond, and the silence smothered him. Finally, he could take it no more. "Have I done something to upset you, Amy? Me or the girls?"

"The girls? You? No, not at all, Mike." Her eyes searched his. "Why?"

"You're distracted. I sense something's up, and I just want to get it out in the open."

Her gaze lowered to her lap, and he watched her weave her fingers together before she looked up again. "It's not you. Grams said something to me that hasn't set well."

He couldn't stop his frown. "Your grandmother?"

"She's worried about you and the girls. You know how—"

"Worried? About what?"

She pressed her lips together, and he could see she

struggled to respond. "She thinks we're close, and she fears that when I go back to Chicago that—"

"That we'll miss you." *When I go back.* A knot rose in his throat.

"Yes, but more than that. I know the girls like me a lot, and—" She squirmed against the chair. "They've already lost someone important to them. I'm—"

"Their mother. Yes, but…"

"Grams worries that they'll be hurt if I go."

If I go. Which was it? *When* or *if?* "You are planning to go back then?" He held his breath waiting for her response. He feared it was too late to guard his heart, or the girls'.

"Yes. No." She shook her head as if trying to toss a wasp from her hair. "I don't know, Mike. I've made a commitment here until June. I don't know if I can find a teaching job in Chicago or if I'll ever have a job here either, so it's a toss-up what will happen."

A ragged breath escaped him. What about the girls and him? Did she even care?

Her gaze softened. "I'll miss all of you terribly if I go back. That's not even a question."

"What draws you back, then—other than the city itself?"

An expression slid across her face that he couldn't read, almost as if she were waiting for her answer to his question.

"You told me you don't have anyone special in your life. I assume that also means no special guy."

She blinked as if he'd surprised her. "I'm not one for dating and romance. You've probably noticed."

Noticed? Never. She'd drawn him to her like a magnet. "Why not? You're a beautiful woman."

She gave her head a quick wag as she lowered her gaze. "Thank you. People say I look like my mom."

"She died, right?"

"Died? Yes, a year ago, but she was gone long before that."

"Gone?"

"One day, she packed her bags and left. She left my dad and me behind. Just walked away."

The bottom fell out of his stomach. "Amy, I'm sorry. I can't even..." His head rattled with empty words. "I don't know what to say."

"Neither did I for years. I was about four when she left."

"Four." And the woman didn't take her child with her? When it sank in, he understood so much. "And you thought you'd done something to send her away."

Looking surprised, she seemed to search for a response.

His chest knotted, facing the hurt he'd caused by making that statement.

"You're right, Mike. I guess that's what I felt. No one else's mother left their child behind and walked away from her home and family."

"You were only four. I'm sure she loved you." He couldn't imagine the hurt and damage she'd experienced. So many questions were answered by her explanation. He sat dumbfounded.

"Maybe she did love me. I'll never know." She lifted her shoulders. "But I deal with it. At least I try."

"But not as well as you'd like." In her eyes, he saw his girls. Their mother had died, but the abandonment they must have felt—maybe still did—overwhelmed him.

Instead of being upset with him, Amy gave a soft chuckle. "You're intuitive, like Grams."

"Am I?"

She nodded. "You have an amazing heart, Mike. It's all in your face."

He'd spent much of his life trying to camouflage his feelings. Had he failed or could it be that Amy had the power to read his emotions better than anyone? And because she read his thoughts, why not finish his thoughts? "And that's why you empathize with the twins."

Her lips pressed together. "Yes, the girls…and you, too. I saw the hurt my father went through. He never totally healed until he got word from her sister that she'd died. After Mom walked out, Dad had little contact with her family and none as time passed." She drew in a lengthy breath. "I barely remember my mother's face, and Dad destroyed all the photos."

The pictures of Laura he'd clung to but had never had the courage to look at surged into his mind. Did the girls still remember what their mom looked like?

An icy sensation rolled through his chest. Had he caused their mother's memory to fade?

"Daddy, look."

Following the cry, footsteps pounded on the hardwood floors, and he turned toward the doorway. The girls charged in each clutching a cloth picture like a December calendar with each day a pocket. He pulled his emotions in place and listened to their explanation of the symbols for each day that attached with velcro.

Ivy pulled out a candle. "See this one, Daddy? It means Jesus is the light of the world. Gramma Ellie made a pocket for every day right up to Christmas."

"That's quite a gift."

Amy eyed the felt calendar. "It's lovely, and each day you'll have a reminder about what Jesus means to you."

Her voice softened as she finished, and Mike noticed the look on her face. Sometimes he could read her, too, and today he saw that she'd almost forgotten what Jesus could do for her. He prayed for her daily that Christ would become a flame in her life. He gazed at the candle in Holly's hand. Everyone needed light in their life. When he looked at Amy, for him, she'd become part of the glow.

Chapter Seven

Mike's mind spun trying to organize the events on Saturday. Christmas in the Village offered more activities than the day could hold. The girls looked forward to going to the library where they could visit with Santa and work on a craft. Amy's interest tended toward visiting the Holiday Bazaar at Maria Hall. He longed to hide out in the Harrisville Arts Council building and enjoy the hot cider and Christmas cookies.

"Aren't we going on a hayride?"

Ivy's voice split his thoughts. "We can't do everything."

Her why-not expression caused him to chuckle. "This is Am—Miss Carroll's first Christmas in the Village. She should get first pick."

The twins eyed each other and for once didn't pout.

Amy perused the flyer listing every event. "I say we head for the library first."

"Yeah." Holly clapped her hands. "The library."

Ivy's eyes widened as a grin grew on her face. "Okay, let's go, and then the hayride." She grasped Amy's hand and gave a tug.

Amy tucked the flier into her bag and fell into step with the girls.

Mike followed behind, seeing something wonderful happening to the twins. They had been pretty well-behaved in her class since the day they missed the bus, and their obvious affection for Amy couldn't go without notice. Even though her grandmother hadn't given her any tips, Amy came by a knack for dealing with the girls naturally. She charmed everyone. Especially him.

But he couldn't let his concern drop. If and when she would return to Chicago wavered on his mind as much as Amy's own indecision. He'd hoped her feelings for them might weigh on her decision, but as yet he hadn't noticed that happening. The disappointment clung as strong as the flooring adhesive his employer sold.

He herded the twins and Amy into the car and headed for the library fifteen miles away. When they arrived, the parking lot was filled, and inside, he stood knee-deep in children waiting to see Santa.

Mike pointed to the far side of the large room. "How about doing your craft first and then meeting Santa?"

Holly's gaze lingered on the man in the red suit before she followed Ivy across the room.

He followed Amy over to the children's corner where the twins had found a spot at the craft table. "What's with the cookies?"

Amy chuckled. "They're tree ornaments made from a kind of cookie dough. The girls can decorate them."

He tried to get a better look at the various cookie-like shapes: gingerbread men, Christmas trees, stars and candlesticks. "I'll admit these cookie things are new to me."

"They're perfect for an old-fashioned Christmas tree."

He cocked his head. "I'm happy to put up a table-top tree with store-bought ornaments."

"Tabletop tree?" Her eyes narrowed. "That's all you have for the girls?"

Her look made him feel a little bit guilty. "They're okay with it."

She closed her eyes as she shook her head. "Every child loves a big Christmas tree."

"Maybe so, but—"

She lifted her index finger. "This year you'll put up a full-size tree."

His pulse bolted. "I will?" She wasn't smiling and neither was he. Her face reflected the same determination he often saw on Holly's face.

"Don't you have woods behind your house? We can cut one down."

The only thing he liked was the "we" part. "You mean put up a live tree?"

"A real tree with all the decorations."

He hadn't decorated a big tree since Laura died, yet today the thought of setting up a tree with Amy inspired him to give it serious thought. He shrugged again. "We'll see."

She grinned at him, a determined look on her face, and he had the feeling she wasn't going to back down. Then it struck him, and his Scrooge attitude fell away. "Did your dad put up a Christmas tree when you were a girl?"

The grin faded. "Never."

Mike's heart twinged. "So it's important to you."

"It's important for the twins. They need to know there's nothing wrong with them. They can have a Christmas tree like everyone else."

Like everyone else. The girls' words flooded his mind. *We're all we got.* His excuses fluttered away. "We'll have a tree."

He settled into silence, and as they watched the girls decorate the cookies, his gaze drifted to Amy's amazing face, her dark hair hanging down her back like Rapunzel, the storybook princess he'd often read about with the girls. He imagined climbing the castle tower to rescue her, clinging to her thick hair. Rescue her? He was the one being rescued by the beautiful princess.

Holly finished first, an angel with a slightly crooked

halo, and Mike glanced at the line for Santa, which continued to grow. He nodded to Amy. She looked at the crowd of children and shrugged. When Ivy finished, Amy was the first to admire her bell with an elaborate bow.

Mike girded his determination, hoping the twins would see his logic. "If you want to go on the hayride, we should go back to town, otherwise we might miss the last trip."

"But what about Santa?" Ivy's face skewed with her question.

"Well, I…" He gave a desperate look at Amy.

She didn't pick up his plea for a moment, and when he'd about given up, her eyes brightened. "Ivy, here's an idea. Why don't you and Holly write letters to Santa and tell him what you'd like for Christmas. That way he won't forget because he has it written on the paper."

"He'll remember better?" Ivy gazed up at Mike.

"He sure will. Things in writing are important."

Holly agreed, but then she leaned closer and whispered, "I don't think that's really Santa anyway. He looks like Mr. Whitman from the pharmacy in a costume."

Mike clamped his teeth together, muting his laughter. He couldn't look at Amy, knowing she'd done the same.

Holly bounded ahead, and Ivy gave a lingering look at Mr. Whitman before following her sister.

Slipping to Amy's side, Mike released a deep breath. "That was close, and thanks for the letter-to-Santa idea."

"Holly's one of a kind. You know that, right? And you're welcome." She tucked her arm in his. "The ornaments gave me an idea. I think I'll teach the kids in my class about old-fashioned Christmases."

Her face glowed, and he wished he could be in her class to learn just about anything.

The hay wagon horses stomped their feet against the hard ground, and Amy shivered with the cold. She wanted to go shopping, but the girls had their hearts set on the hayride. She couldn't disappoint them. Mike had grabbed a blanket from his car as they headed inside the Arts Council building, which smelled of cider and sugar cookies. Although the hot drink warmed her and the cookies were a hit with Mike and his daughters, they marched into the chilly weather to get in line too soon.

Waiting for her turn to climb on the wagon, she eyed the handsome team of horses, roan-colored with flowing white manes. The cowboy helping the crowd onto the wagon took his time, and finally when they reached the portable steps, the girls scampered up first before Mike helped her onto the wagon bed. She settled on the rough hay and braced herself for the ride. Wondering about the girls, she craned her neck and saw them leaning over the railing, and as the horses moved ahead, an urge grew. "Save my spot. I want to check on the girls."

"Okay." He gave her a curious grin as she leaned on him to rise.

She worked her way around feet and bodies until she reached the twins, and when they noticed her, surprise lit their faces.

"We can see the horses from here." Holly's eyes glistened.

She gazed at the team. "They're pretty." Her intent moved her to slip her arm around their shoulders. "I want to tell you how much I've enjoyed being with you today. You've been really good, and I like that."

A smile slipped to their faces. Ivy lifted her arm and touched Amy's hand. "We like you with us."

Her pulse skipped. "You do?"

Holly nodded. "It's like having a mom."

Amy's chest constricted, and her heart melted. "Can I tell you a story about me?"

"When you were a girl?" Holly's eager face mirrored Ivy's.

"I didn't have a mom either when I grew up. She went away when I was four, and she died a year ago. So I know what it's like not having a mom."

Holly shifted closer. "Do you still remember her?"

Amy's answer wavered in her mind. "She's still in my heart and thoughts."

"I remember my mom, too, but sometimes I forget what she looked like."

Ivy's confession rent her heart.

Holly nestled closer to Amy's side. "I try to remember her really hard."

"You will always remember. Moms are always in our hearts."

Relief swept over their faces.

Amy gave them a quick hug, then asked, "Will you be very careful here if you stay by the railing?"

They nodded.

"Okay. Your dad and I are over there." She pointed to where Mike was seated. He saw them and waved back. "Hang on tight." She maneuvered through the others to return to Mike. She grasped his shoulder. "The girls promised to be careful."

He grinned and helped her down, this time drawing her back against his chest.

Warm and comfortable, she savored the moment. The clop of hooves echoed on the road to the state park, and the breeze turned colder sending a chill through her even with the warmth of the blanket spread over her lap.

Mike slipped his arms around her. "Is this better?"

Although her indecision about the future nipped at her, Mike's nearness warmed her. "Much. Thanks."

He leaned closer, his cheek resting against her hair. "You keep me warm, too."

A Bible verse nudged its way from the recesses of her mind. *Two are better than one…* The specific wording failed her but another line expressed that two can keep warm, but how can one keep warm alone? Today the question became real. Was that the completeness that Grams had talked about?

Weighted with thought, only the hum of nearby conversations and the steady rhythm of the horses' hooves broke the quiet until someone in the crowd began to sing "Jingle Bells." The music drew her from her darker thoughts, and her spirit lifted when Mike's voice blended in song. She admired his full baritone voice.

She rarely sang, but she joined in. Mike gave her a squeeze and leaned over to send her a smile, and she was filled with contentment.

When the last verse ended, Mike broke into "Deck the Halls." Others chimed in, some in harmony, while others clapped in rhythm. Her heart soared. Today she knew what Grams meant when she talked about fullness. An ethereal sensation wove through her body and sent her to a place she had never known.

After the second verse, Mike ended the song, and before another began, Amy tilted her head to see his face. "You make me happy."

His eyes glinted. "I'm glad." He leaned forward and kissed her.

The warm touch sent a flurry of heartbeats skittering through her chest. The scent of hay, the sweet cookies, the brisk breeze, the music and the tender kiss permeated her senses. The warmth lingered as the horses slowed and returned to the Harrisville Arts Council building, though her mind kept returning to the girls' question: Do you still remember your mother?

When she got off the wagon, Holly and Ivy chattered about the ride but made it clear they were eager to get home.

Mike sent Ivy a questioning look. "Why are you so anxious to leave?"

She leaned against his hip. "I'm hungry."

"Me, too." Holly stood back, a determined look growing on her face. "And we don't want to go shopping."

Amy couldn't stop laughing. "So that's the problem." Even though Mike's face darkened, she signaled him to say nothing. "Let's see if they can stay with Grams for a little while. Would that be fun?"

The girls agreed but Mike only shrugged. "If you think she won't mind."

"She'll love it." She pulled out her cell phone, knowing Grams would say yes, and she and Mike could shop without interruption.

Mike stood back and observed Amy's profile as she made a purchase at one of the booths in Maria Hall. No matter how many times he tried to understand why she'd remained single, nothing made sense. Everything about her attracted him—her hair, her bright eyes, her lithe figure. And best of all, she had an innate wisdom and admirable sensitivity and compassion for others. Beauty and brains.

Amy turned from the booth and sent him a teasing

grin. "I've never seen so many handcrafted items in my life. I love it." She rubbed her shoulder against his. "But you're bored."

He loved spending time with her. But not shopping. "I'm not bored. I'm hungry." He motioned to the food area. "They serve lunch here if you want to take a break."

"Sounds good to me." She slipped beside him, and he linked his arm through hers as they headed toward the scent of hot dogs.

With their snack on a tray, he steered her toward a table. Once seated, he dug into the food, but Amy seemed more excited about her purchases.

She delved into one of her bags and brought out a pinecone ornament. "See this?"

He nodded.

"Here's my idea. I know how to make these, and Grams has a basket of pinecones she's saved. We can teach the girls how to make ornaments, and they can have an old-fashioned Christmas tree. I'm going to do this with my class, too." She grinned at him. "It'll be fun."

Her exuberance tickled him. "It sounds great except the part where you said *we*. I have no idea how to make anything like that."

"I'll teach you." She shifted her hand close to his and pressed it. "I think the girls will feel proud to help, and when they do something positive, it's a great time to compliment them." Her face grew serious. "Did you ever think about this? Kids misbehave when they don't get enough positive attention. So they've learned that being naughty gets them noticed."

He thought about how he reacted to the girls. "You always have the answers." But for some reason his hot dog sat in his stomach like a rock.

Amy became thoughtful, and he waited. "If you don't mind more ideas, I have another one."

Her sidelong glance made him nervous, but he opted to listen. "Sure."

"The girls said something on the hayride that bothered me a lot. They miss their mother, and their greatest fear is that they'll forget what she looked like."

Her comment struck a sore spot. "How did this come up?"

"They told me today that when I was with them, they felt like they had a mom again." As she explained their conversation to Mike, her voice began to tremble.

"I saw some picture frames at Maggie's On Main when we were in there, and I think that would be a great gift for their birthday. You could give them a photograph of their mom."

He lowered his eyes, frustrated by his lack of awareness. "The other day they asked me if I still thought of Laura, and later I thought about the photos of her I'd tucked away and hadn't the courage to look at. I've cheated the girls, haven't I?" He found the strength to lift his head and look at Amy.

"Not cheated. Not at all. You didn't throw them away as my dad did." Her gaze captured his. "You can still fix it."

He forced a smile and agreed, but in his heart, Mike wondered if he truly could.

Chapter Eight

Amy sat in her room, gazing at her purchases and thinking about her conversation with Mike. She suspected she'd hurt his feelings and now felt badly about it. Another thing had dawned on her. She loved his daughters far more than she should. Their loss brought back hers, the old ache she'd lived with ever since she could remember. When she thought of Mike and the photos, she was grateful he hadn't closed off the girls to their mother the way her father had done.

The wagon ride flashed through her mind—and the kiss—and she relived her confusing emotions. If she had any plans to leave Harrisville, she had to distance herself from them, but when she considered it, she felt empty. Her mind wrestled with her heart. Somewhere inside her lay the truth, and she needed to find it.

The Bible verse "Two are better than one" jogged her mind again. That was how she'd felt since she met Mike—the kind of completeness that Grams talked about. She dug into one of the bags and drew out a full apron and matching potholders. Her grandmother would love it when the gift came from the twins. Grams spent so much time in the kitchen with them, teaching them to cook. Her, too. The memory eased her tension.

She grasped the pinecone ornament and opened her bedroom door. Instead of the kitchen, for once Grams sat in an easy chair in the living room flipping through a magazine. "Look what I bought." She held up the decoration.

Grams nodded. "It's pretty. Some people can do a lot with a pinecone."

"You have a basket of them in the garage. Can I use them?" She held her breath.

"Why not? We used to toss them into the fireplace as kindling, but I rarely use the fireplace anymore." A sadness slipped Grams, then vanished.

Tenderness and concern for her rose up in Amy. "You're thinking of Gramps?"

She nodded, an easy smile returning to her lips. "I always do this time of year." She shifted forward in the chair and pushed herself up. "That reminds me of something." She held up her index finger and shuffled from the room.

Amy's curiosity grew as she sank into Gramps' old recliner.

When her grandmother returned, she held papers in her hand. "The girls mentioned they didn't talk with Santa today and asked if they could write him a letter. I guess you suggested it?"

She nodded. "I did. The line was too long, and we would have missed the hayride." Amy recalled Mike's closeness and their kiss.

Grams handed her the letters. "I think you should read them."

Amy studied Grams's face as she clasped the paper. She gazed at the first letter and read the words, her heart in her throat.

Dear Santa, My daddy isn't happy and neither are me and Holly. So I want a mom for our family. If you'd let me pick her out, I would pick Miss Carroll, my second grade teacher.

Love, Ivy Russet

Holly's letter was pretty much identical to Ivy's.

Tears welled in her eyes and rolled down her cheeks. She lifted her gaze to her grandmother and drew a ragged breath. "This breaks my heart."

Grams only nodded, tears evident in her eyes as well. "That's what I said to you the other day. These little girls feel your love, and they'll be heartbroken if you leave."

"I didn't mean this to happen, Grams. I..." Amy covered her face with her hands and let the tears flow.

Her grandmother shuffled closer and patted her back. "God has a way, Amy. Put it in His hands. But just be careful of their little hearts." She released a sigh. "And Mike's, too."

The more her grandmother said, the more she ached for Mike and the twins. It wasn't pity, but something far deeper. Something inside her, too. Prayer was always Grams's answer, and if anyone knew the Lord, it was her grandmother. "I'll pray, Grams. I'm up to my neck in their lives. I'll think of something."

"With God's help, you will."

Amy handed the girls' letters back to her.

Grams tucked them in her apron pocket. "I thought I'd give these to Mike, but after I read them, I wasn't sure…"

"Right. Please don't." Concern rolled through her.

"Trust me, child. I don't want to do any more damage than there already is."

Damage. The word pierced her. She'd never thought of her time with Mike and the girls as damage. "I don't know what to do. The girls are in my class, so I see them every day, and they live so close." She massaged her forehead between her eyes. "I've promised to help with their Christmas tree, too."

"You have a responsibility now. Let your heart and God's leading be your guide."

Her stomach knotted. She cared about the girls. She found Mike to be the image of the perfect husband, but God's leading? Prayer? This time she needed to listen to her grandmother.

"I have something that might help you." Grams scuffed out of the room, her slippers making a swishing noise on the carpet. She soon returned with a small booklet in her hand. "My daily devotion." She waved the tract in the air. "Listen to this. It struck me that it has meaning for you." She opened the folder. "It's from *Acts* 2:28. 'You have made known to me the paths of life; you will fill me with joy in your presence.'" She lifted her head and searched Amy's face.

"I don't know my paths of life, Grams. I have to figure them out." She'd expected a sensible solution, something she could do that would make a difference.

"But you will when you listen to Him. And what about the joy? What brought you joy in Chicago? Think about that, child. What brings you joy now? Here?"

Grams's questions knocked Amy flat. She fell back against the recliner. Joy in Chicago? Her job teaching. Her friends. Joy in Harrisville? Her job teaching, yes, but other things gave her greater joy. Watching the twins' behavior improve. Hearing them giggle. Hearing Mike sing. Seeing his smile. Enjoying the kiss they'd shared. Feeling complete. The realization stunned her.

"Dear Lord, am I hearing You, or is it my own crazy thoughts?" She looked up to heaven and prayed.

* * *

Amy looked out the window at the sunshine and the snowless ground. In good weather, recess gave her time to prepare for the next lesson, and today, she looked forward to their social studies class. She'd added an art project, because today the class would bring to life what they'd been learning about Christmas in the past—Victorian times, and the Great Depression in the 1930s when money was low but creativity was high.

The bell rang, and she geared herself for the onslaught of students. Noises resounded in the hall as they hung up their heavy coats. The seats began to fill with eager seven-year-olds, eyeing the equipment she had stacked on her desk, but Holly and Ivy hadn't appeared yet. Her concern rose, then dissipated when Ivy charged into the room, her face marred by a frown. Holly ambled in behind her and sat in her seat.

Ivy slowed when she reached her desk. She leaned over and whispered, "Holly did a bad thing."

"What was it?"

"She told me some of the girls were playing hide and seek, and I was It." She glanced over her shoulder at Holly, whose face now carried a similar frown.

"And?"

"But no one came to find me. I waited and waited, and then a third-grader told me no one was looking for me. Holly was playing tag with some of the girls."

Amy's chest constricted as she beckoned to Holly,

who took her time to join Ivy at her desk. "I'm very disappointed."

Holly's frown sank to feigned innocence. "Why?"

"I've been so proud of both of you getting along so well, and now look what happened."

Holly elbowed Ivy. "It was a joke."

Ivy poked her back. "Not very funny."

Amy slipped between them and knelt. "It's only funny when both people are laughing. Is Ivy laughing?"

Holly gave her a look and shook her head.

"Holly, please say you're sorry because I love being proud of you."

Holly seemed to think it over a moment before her face displayed her defeat. "I'm sorry."

Amy's heart jolted when she gave Ivy a hug, though her disappointment at the setback remained. "Thank you. Now get to your seats because we're having a fun project today."

Both of them scrutinized her desk before settling into their seats.

Amy walked around the classroom with a stack of old newspapers and slipped one on each desk. "We've been learning about old-fashioned Christmases, and today, we're going to make an old-fashioned tree ornament."

The room buzzed with the children's excitement as they craned their necks to see what else she had in store for them.

"Everyone will cover the desk with newspaper. I have a few bottles of craft glue that we have to share, some ribbon and a pinecone for everyone." She held one up. "You see these all over the ground under the evergreen trees."

"Miss Carroll." A child waved her hand from the back of the room. "I have those in my yard."

"Once you learn to make these, perhaps your mom will allow you to make more for your tree. I'll send everyone home with instructions."

"Yeah!"

When she'd finished distributing the paper, the students got up from their seats and gathered around her desk. "First watch me as I make one, and then I'll let you pick out your packets of glitter and we'll share the glue. Be careful and don't get this on your clothing. Okay?"

They nodded as they gathered around to watch her drizzle the pinecone with glue, letting it drip down the sides and then sprinkle on the glitter. As it dried, she made a bow from the ribbon and attached it to the top with more glue. Finally she used wire to make a tree hook. "Can you do this?"

Their voices blended in agreement, and they scurried back to their desks to begin.

Amy walked up and down the rows, handing each child a pinecone. As she moved around the room, she kept track of Holly and Ivy, but her fears ended when she saw them working together as if nothing had happened. Her hope rose and so did her enthusiasm as she observed the children's excitement.

Her mind stole back to Sunday when she'd finally gone to church with Grams. But her guilt doubled, seeing her grandmother's happiness and knowing until that day she'd never gone with her. Church attendance meant everything to her, and it seemed sitting beside Grams, she'd given her a gift.

The sermon about being ready and prepared for Jesus held meaning, but a young woman's solo touched her most, a song called "Breath of Heaven" about Mary's difficult journey to Bethlehem. When she listened to the message of Mary waiting in prayer and wondering if she could carry her burden, Amy's mind shifted to her own problems and prayers. Mary prayed for strength and understanding, and pleaded with the Lord to stay near her. The same words wrought in Amy's heart.

Since Sunday, she'd thought a lot about her faith. She believed in Jesus, but she'd stepped away from Him. She'd turned her back, but the song helped her realize that asking God for help was the only way to deal with her confusion.

A sound at the door broke her thought. She turned, surprised to see the principal beckoning to her. Her stomach twisted, fearing she would have to defend her art project as part of Social Studies, but the kids were having fun and learning, and Christmas was so close.

Amy made her way to the doorway and stepped into the hall, leaving the door open so she could check on the children. "Is something wrong?"

Mrs. Fredericks grinned. "Not with you." She nodded toward the classroom. "What are they doing?"

She explained the project before beginning her apology.

"This is a great idea, Amy. You're so creative. I noticed how the children are focused and working so well together. Look at Timmy over there helping Duncan. Those two don't always get along."

Amy's concern fluttered away when the expected reprimand became a compliment. "Thank you, and I've been working on getting those two boys more civil."

"You're doing a great job. And with the twins, too." She eased farther from the door. "I have some news for you. I could have waited to talk with you, but I really wanted you to hear this."

Her pulse picked up pace. "What news?"

"Mrs. Larch's baby was born premature. They're both fine, but she's decided to take more time off from teaching to spend time with the child." She gave Amy a tender look. "Sometimes priorities change."

"They do. I'm sorry to hear about Mrs. Larch." She studied the principal's face trying to decide why she'd told her. "I suppose you'd like me to tell the children?"

"No." She held up her hand. "Let's not confuse

them. They'll be moving on to third grade next year and by then it won't mean so much that she's not back."

"Yes, that makes sense." But this didn't make sense until a thread of possibility wove through her mind. Would this mean—?

"So under the circumstances, I'm offering you the second grade class for next year."

"Next year? You mean you'd like me to return in September?"

"Yes, if you're willing. You don't have to answer today if you don't want to. I'll give you time to consider the proposal, but you're doing a tremendous job, and I would be thrilled to have you join the staff."

"Don't you have to get approval for this—"

Mrs. Fredericks's flexed hand charged upward again. "Naturally I talked to the superintendent and those who make the decisions in the administrative office. I've told them about your work here, and they are pleased with my choice."

"Thank you for your confidence." Dumbfounded by the offer, Amy's mind lurched with questions. "It sounds wonderful, but I would like to think about it. It will mean finding a permanent place to live." She was sure her grandmother would invite her to stay, but she needed time to think.

Mrs. Fredericks's face darkened. "I'd hoped you'd be eager to say yes, but I understand. Take the time you need."

Amy wished she could look happier, but the dilemma spun in her mind.

"Could you give us an answer after Christmas? That will give you time to make a decision. If you decline, then we can advertise the opening next semester."

Touched by her kindness, Amy managed a smile. "I'm pleased you have confidence in me and it's a wonderful offer. Don't worry, I'll make the decision by then."

She gave her a thumbs-up. "Good job in there with those kids. I can't believe how quiet they are." She turned and headed back down the hallway.

Amy gazed into the room, thrilled the project had been such a success. But the success took a backseat to her bewilderment. She'd prayed for God to make her path known. Had the Lord answered her already?

Chapter Nine

Mike gave the chili a stir and walked to the window. The milder weather had taken a vacation, and a nippy wind returned, rattling the shutters and playing with the shingles. Northern Michigan residents had learned to deal with the hard winters, but could Amy? He knew Chicago was called the Windy City, but it wasn't the wind but long-winded politicians who gave the city its reputation—at least that's how the story went.

Amy had been busy since Christmas In The Village. They'd had a wonderful time that day, he'd thought, but he hadn't seen her since, and it had turned his brain to mush. He knew better than to open his heart to someone who might not be sticking around. But then he'd learned the heart had a mind of its own.

Tonight she'd given him hope. She'd called to ask

if she could come over and make the Christmas tree ornaments she'd promised the girls. He'd purchased everything she'd asked—whole cranberries, popcorn, construction paper and glue.

The twins insisted on going outside to search for pinecones. He'd admired the two sparkly ones they'd brought home from school, and he guessed they'd be making more of those. Creativity seemed to be something Amy enjoyed. The only thing he could do was show off his cooking. He'd invited her to dinner. He might not be a top chef, but he'd learned his way around a kitchen.

His pulse quickened when he heard footsteps on the porch. He headed for the door only to be disillusioned when he saw his daughter.

Holly hurried in, with Ivy at her heels. "It's cold out there."

"We nearly froze our fingers off." Ivy held up her hands rosy from the cold.

"Where are your gloves?"

"The pinecones are sticky, so we took them off."

He studied both girls. "Okay, but where are the pinecones?"

"We left them out by the tree." Holly pointed in the direction of the woods. "We need a box to carry them."

"After dinner, we'll go out and get them." He pointed to the chili pot. "Take off your coats."

Another sound caught his attention, and this time he saw Amy waving at him through the window. He opened the door and she came in. "I think I'm getting a real taste of northern winter."

He hated to tell her this was only the beginning. "You're just in time for dinner." He motioned toward the kitchen table. "We'll eat here if that's okay."

"It's great. Can I help?"

"Everything's taken care of. Have a seat." He beckoned to the girls. "Wash your hands."

They hurried off to the bathroom while he opened the oven and pulled out a pan of cornbread.

Amy watched him with a look of amusement as he dished up the chili and sliced the cornbread. Later he'd surprise her with his homemade cherry pie.

In moments, the twins slipped into their chairs and he joined them. He stretched out his arm, and Holly grasped his hand and Ivy's.

Amy took a moment before she caught on. She slipped her hand into Ivy's and then his. They bowed their heads as he said the blessing, his senses coming alive, as he felt her chilly hand resting in his palm. When he released it, she took a moment before lifting her spoon and taking a bite.

"Great chili, Mike. I didn't know you were such a good cook."

He smiled. "Thanks, and don't miss the cornbread. It's homemade."

She dished a square onto the plate, slathered it with butter and tasted it, giving him a thumbs-up.

Ivy lowered her spoon. "We found some pinecones today."

"You did?" Amy swung her gaze from one twin to the other. "Thank you. We need them. I used up all Grams's for the class."

Holly nodded. "We know."

The girls quieted, and when Mike offered the pie, Amy declined. "I couldn't eat another bite. Is later okay?"

Mike nodded and rose to carry the empty bowls to the sink. Amy followed with the plates and leftover cornbread, and while she rinsed, he loaded the dishwasher. Mike remembered what life was like with a partner. Even mundane chores became a pleasure. He wiped his hand on a dish towel and hung it on the rack. "I need to go outside with the girls to pick up the pinecones."

Before he could suggest she wait inside, she headed for her coat. "We can look for a Christmas tree in the woods while we're out."

"To cut today?"

"Not today. Saturday is good. Hopefully it'll be warmer."

The girls grabbed their coats while he located the box he used to carry the groceries. He slipped on his boots and coat, then returned to the kitchen.

Carrying the carton, he opened the door, and the twins and Amy filed outside and down the porch steps. The chill hit him as he closed the door, but Amy's enthusiasm motivated him to face the elements.

The girls ran ahead toward their stash, and he

caught up with Amy. "Haven't seen you much lately. I've missed you."

She lowered her head as she walked. "I've had some things to take care of, and to be honest, some decisions to make."

Decisions? The word left him colder than the weather. Her voice sounded heavy and even uncertain, and though he wanted to ask, he was also afraid to hear her answer. "Can I help?"

She shook her head. "No, I—" She shrugged. "It's complicated." She lifted her face to him. "Can we talk about it another time?"

"Sure. Whatever makes you happy."

"That's what I'm trying to figure out." Her voice seemed a whisper. "I'm happy here. I know that, but will I always be?"

Her question left him disappointed and without a response.

When she looked at him, her expression had changed. "I don't want to talk about that now. Let's get the pinecones."

Hearing her unexpected lighthearted tone, he tucked his arm through hers, and they hurried toward the girls. When he dropped the container on the ground, they attacked the pile and tossed in the pinecones.

Amy moved ahead. "Here's a bunch." She beckoned for the box and then moved on again. Once the last cone had been gathered, she stood over the box. "That's enough, I think."

A plan brewed in Mike's head. "Girls, you run these in and wash the sap off your hands. We'll join you in a few minutes."

With no argument, they skittered off, toting the box. Mike paused a moment in the dusky light. "You want to see the trees we have?"

She gazed into the thicker woods. "We spent so much time collecting pinecones, I'm afraid it's too dark now."

He pointed to the full moon. "There's enough light, I think." His motivation grew as they headed toward the darkness. Trees were his last concern. Stars splashed across the sky, and the moon shed a pale glow along the path. "Be careful." He slipped his hand into hers.

She didn't resist as they headed into the cluster of fir trees.

He gathered his thoughts. "Anything going on I should know? Is something wrong?"

He felt her flinch. "Not wrong." She stopped and turned to face him. "I think you'd be happy."

"Happy?" His pulse escalated. "What is it?"

"I've been offered a permanent teaching position at the school."

"What?" He slipped his arms around her and pulled her to him. "That's wonderful."

"It should be."

His heart sank at her words. "You're not excited?"

"No, I am, but…" She drew back. "I don't know."

He searched her shadowed face. "You don't know if you can stay here, in a small town."

She nodded. "Right now it's great. It's sort of like I'm home, but this isn't my normal lifestyle. Can I be happy without malls where I can shop and theaters where I can see plays?"

They had places to shop in Oscoda. Not big stores like Chicago, but she would have choices. And stage plays? Alpena had a civic theater, and the high school put on a couple plays each year. "Are those the things that make you happy?"

"They did, Mike, but now…I'm not sure. I'm so confused."

Confused. So was he.

The moonlight glinted off her cheek, and he spied a rivulet of tears rolling down her face. He felt horrible knowing he'd made her cry with his questions.

She nestled closer.

Mike tightened his grip, his heart prodding him to act. He raised his finger and followed the line of her tears to her chin, then tilted it upward and kissed the moisture from her cheeks. As he did, her lips drew nearer, touching his. He drank in the sweetness, and even though the crisp air whisked past, the cold vanished as Amy's fingers brushed along the nape of his neck. As her tension ebbed away, he drew his lips from hers, having so much to say but remaining silent.

Amy breathed a lengthy sigh. "So much for the tree."

His chuckle followed hers, and before they turned back, Holly's voice reached them on the wind. "Daddy, where are you? Are we making an old-fashioned Christmas tree or not?"

When her hand slipped from his neck, he prayed the kiss would help her make her decision.

The kiss. Amy leaned back against her pillow. She hadn't been kissed like that for years, not since she'd made her decision that romantic relationships weren't worth the trouble. The kisses of the past had always seemed empty, emotionless. Not last night. Mike's kiss filled her with an amazing feeling of connection and awareness.

Mike understood her. He asked the right questions, his responses soothed her and he made her laugh. They'd known each other such a short time, but it felt like forever. And the girls. Despite Holly's slip back into her bad behavior tricking Ivy with a false hide-and-seek game, the girls were behaving very well.

She'd learned what they needed. Love and attention. When she became sidetracked, and she had been distracted that day at school, that's when they acted badly. Mike needed to give each twin quality time separately.

When Mike had asked her what made her happy, she'd mentioned shopping and the theater. But when she truly thought about it, those things were just moments in time. They pleased her but they weren't lasting. Relationships brought happiness. Mike stood by his promises. She knew it deep in her heart.

She sat up in bed, threw her legs over the mattress and slipped on her robe. When she opened her bedroom door, the scent of coffee greeted her. Noises from the kitchen told her Grams was cooking. Breakfast or baked goods? When Amy stepped through the doorway, a frying pan of scrambled eggs answered her question.

Grams turned. "Good. You're up." She opened the oven and pulled out a plate of bacon.

"You're too good to me." Amy headed for the coffeepot and poured a cup before sliding onto a chair at the table. She took a sip, letting her thoughts sort themselves. When her grandmother glanced her way, she let one question surface. "Can people change?"

Her grandmother drew back. "What people?"

She chuckled. "Me."

"In what way?"

Her shoulder lifted in a shrug.

Grams placed the bacon on the table and scooped the eggs onto two plates before she answered. "I think change is part of life. Things happen—technology, inventions, values."

"Values." She wrapped her mind around the word.

"You're still weighing your decision about the

job?" She set a plate in front of Amy and another for herself. "I told you you're welcome to stay here as long as you want. That's not a problem." She sank into a chair and bowed her head to say a blessing. When Grams finished the prayer, she opened her eyes and patted Amy's hand. "But that's not what's bothering you."

It wasn't a question. Grams knew what bothered her. "No. It's getting involved and taking a chance."

A grin eased onto Grams's face. "Taking a chance on love. There's an old song about that." She looked off in the distance and started to hum.

"He kissed me."

Her grandmother made a slow turn. "I assume you mean Mike."

Amy nodded.

"It's about time."

A blush colored Amy's face. "Grams." She dug her fork into the eggs.

"You two were made for each other, Amy. But you need to see that for yourself."

The realization had slipped over her like a wispy cobweb. A small tickle that she brushed away. But trying to make sense of her feelings, the web had become a noose waiting to catch her unaware. Now that had vanished, and all she saw was a wonderful man with two amazing girls.

Yet Mike hadn't dated since his wife died. What made her assume he wanted anything serious? Maybe he only wanted a friend. Or someone to help him with the twins. She sipped her coffee, studying Grams's face and hoping her grandmother's wisdom would brush off on her. "I have until after Christmas to let them know my decision, so I need to give this careful thought. I can't base my decision on Mike or what might happen between us." And she couldn't base her decision on two little girls who asked Santa for a mother. The thought prickled along her spine. She drew in a breath. "I need to learn my purpose, my path. You said that yourself."

"And also what brings you joy."

Joy. The answer slipped across her like a satin sheet, soft and gentle. She knew it wasn't shopping or seeing a play. Last night, as they made ornaments, her heart sang. And when Mike kissed her, she'd been lost in his arms. If that wasn't joy, she didn't know what was.

Chapter Ten

Mike squeezed the glue bottle, watching it drip down the pinecone. He eyed Amy's ornament, admiring her blend of gold and red glitter. Maybe he should do one with blue and silver. The girls had spent the morning, even before Amy arrived, gluing strips of construction paper into loops, one around the other. They'd created a long strand to drape around the tree.

Amy held her ornament in the air, as if admiring it.

He grinned, enjoying her enthusiasm. "Next year you'll have your own booth at Maria Hall." He gave her a wink. "How many more of these things are we going to make?"

She motioned to the few pinecones left. "Let's finish them. It'll be beautiful." She caught the girls' attention at the other end of the dining room table. "And then we'll go out and cut down a tree."

"Yippee!" They clapped their sticky hands and giggled at the mess they'd made.

Mike looked over at the other decorations they'd already made—strings of alternating cranberries and popcorn—and smiled to himself. With Amy, there was never a dull moment. That was one thing he loved about her. He'd adored his wife, but her long illness after the girls were born slowed their time together to a crawl. Still he believed when God brought two people together, they were yoked as one, so each partner's joys or sorrows spread over both.

He gazed at Amy again. She'd been mum about her decision since she'd arrived earlier, and he'd decided to let the subject lie until she was ready to talk. But his prayers continued because he'd admitted the truth. She'd become more than a friend. He was in love with her.

"Look, Daddy."

He swung his gaze to the twins who'd stretched the lengthy chain all the way through the living room doorway and halfway back. "Good job. I'm really proud how well you worked together."

They glowed as they gathered the loops and dropped them onto a living room chair.

Ivy leaned against his shoulder. "Can we pick out a tree now?"

He caught Amy's gaze, and she nodded. He gestured to the bathroom. "Clean your hands first. Then put on your boots and coats. It's been snowing all morning."

"I love snow." Holly bounced past him toward the kitchen where they'd left their gear in the back entry.

Amy admired another of her creations. "I guess we can save the last two for next year." She motioned to the pinecones.

We can. He loved the sound of "we." Yet he cautioned himself from reading too much into her playful comment.

He washed his hands in the kitchen sink, and when he slipped on his boots and coat, he met her by the front door ready to go. They headed outside, the girls running ahead, and Amy following behind them while he darted into the garage to find the saw. He'd cut only one tree from the woods while Laura was alive. After she saw it in the stand, she suggested the next year they purchase one from the lots that was trimmed and shaped. Now he would learn what Amy preferred.

As he headed into the woods, laughter floated past him with the snowflakes. When he found them, all three were sprawled in the snow making snow angels. He stood over them and grinned. "I thought you were picking out a tree."

"Come on, we're having fun." Amy beckoned to him.

Holly sat up and pointed to a sweep of fresh snow. "Make an angel, Daddy."

Amy's laugh tickled him, and he plopped the saw on the ground and flung himself into the powdery crystals and spread his arms and legs as they had done. Happiness seeped through his body as certain as the icy crystals sent a chill to his bones. Before he could rise, Amy and the girls were standing over him, grins spread across their faces.

"I wish I had a camera." Amy held up her hands as if taking a picture. "Maybe next year." Her smile made his heart pitch.

He rose, noticing his giant snow angel compared to the other three, before he beckoned them deeper into the fir trees, treasuring his lighthearted feeling. They each darted in their own direction while he followed their footsteps zigzagging through the evergreens as he nixed Ivy's ten-foot tree and Amy's six-foot-wide one. He listened for Holly's voice and followed her to a stand of beautiful spruces. Behind him, Amy and Ivy bounded to his side, and they all stopped, each gazing at the same tree. The lovely six-foot tree with well-shaped branches looked perfect. "What do you think?" he asked.

Everyone agreed. His spirit high, Mike knelt in the snow and drew the blade across the base, digging deeper into the trunk until he saw it wobble. "Can you catch it, Amy?"

She darted to the far side and grabbed it as it broke loose. "It's perfect."

Holly headed off, her voice sailing back to them. "I'll get the stand, Daddy. I know where it is."

"Me, too."

As Ivy sped away, he stood beside Amy, wrapped

in the greatest joy he'd felt in years. "You've done wonders for those girls. I can't thank you enough."

She rested her hand on his arm. "I can't thank you enough either."

"For what?"

"For being you."

She lowered her eyes a moment, and when she lifted them, Mike looked into their depths and wished he had something brilliant to say. He stood in silence as snowflakes drifted past, catching on her long lashes.

Amy touched his cheek. "And for letting me learn to be me." Her gaze moved to his lips and he answered her with a kiss as the tree sank to the ground. When Amy's arm slipped across his back, he drew her closer, feeling her warmth seeping to his heart.

The kiss broke, but she remained in his embrace.

She tilted her head back, looking in his eyes. "I suppose we'd better get inside. The girls will be out here any minute."

"You know them too well." He grasped the tree trunk and slipped one arm around her back as they moved through the drifting flakes.

Amy stood back admiring the tree and the man who was holding up his daughter so she could place the angel on top. The decision that had weighed on her for so long now seemed a feather.

As she hung the strings of cranberries and popcorn and helped the family drape the long chain of colorful paper hoops around the branches, her mind stayed on their kiss in the snow-covered woods. This blue-and-white house with the loving family inside had taught her more about herself than she'd ever learned on her own.

"What do you think?" Mike moved beside her. "Not bad, huh?"

She gazed at him instead of the tree. "Not bad at all." He grinned, but she wasn't sure if he'd caught on or not.

Ivy dangled a pinecone ornament from her finger. "What about this one?"

"You hid it." Holly put her arms on her hips. "I thought the angel was the last one."

Mike chuckled. "You did a good job putting on the angel, Holly. See how straight and special it is? But Ivy finally pulled a fast one on you." He beckoned her with his index finger. "Let's put on the last pinecone."

She nodded and looked at the tree for a moment before she settled on a place to hang it. "Now it's perfect."

Slipping his arm around Ivy, he drew Holly into an embrace. "Here are my two wonderful girls who are growing up too fast."

As they nestled to his side, Amy stood back, her heart ready to burst. "You all did a good job."

Ivy slipped from beneath Mike's arm and came to her side. "The old-fashioned tree was your idea." She gave Amy a hug.

Tears pulsated behind Amy's eyes. The girls she'd considered bad seeds had become blossoming flowers, thriving on love.

Holly, not to be outdone, skipped toward her, too, and added another hug.

She squeezed back. "Thank you. I had as much fun as you did."

Mike checked his watch. "And now it's time for two young ladies to go to bed." He shooed them away. "You'll see Amy tomorrow at church, right?"

He lifted an eyebrow her way, and she nodded.

He grinned. "How about some coffee and a piece of my homemade pie?" He leaned closer. "And I wanted to talk about," he whispered, "the girls' birthday."

She settled on the sofa, her legs curled beneath her, and her focus on the tree. It had turned out better than she'd imagined, and she wished they had time to make eggshell ornaments. Maybe another year.

Another year. The decision she'd been trying to make had begun to make itself. She leaned her head against the cushion and closed her eyes. Pure comfort. Since she'd arrived in Harrisville, her life had found its own rhythm, slower and steadier but with a great beat. The frenetic pace of Chicago, once under her skin, had lured her with all its excitement, but she'd found a new kind of energy here, an exhilaration she'd never felt before.

"Here you go."

She opened her eyes and found Mike standing over her with the coffee and pie. "Thanks."

A curious look grew on his face. "Thinking?"

She nodded. "About Harrisville, a small town that's made a big impression on me."

He settled beside her. "A big impression? Really?"

"Everything keeps falling into place and I sense the Lord is showing me my path."

He swept his fingers through his hair. "I don't quite understand."

She set her cup on the coffee table. "I've spent years letting my parents' problems hang over me like a shroud, and I think God is telling me to let it go. I couldn't solve their problems years ago, and I can't solve them now. My mom's gone, and my dad's found a new life. And that's what I need. I've decided to stay in Harrisville and make it my home."

He drew back, his eyes widening. "Wow! Amy, I…" His sagging jaw closed to a smile.

"You're speechless."

"I guess I am." He shook his head. "I know you've been struggling with your decision, but today I really hoped… You seem relaxed and—"

"Happy."

"Happy, and now you've made me happy."

She brushed her hand over his cheek. "You deserve to be happy, Mike. You've had a difficult three years, raising two girls alone. Two lovely girls, I might add."

His expression grew tender. "And I give you credit for that."

"I did a few things that helped, I suppose, but you're a wonderful dad." She gave his cheek a gentle touch. "I'm anxious to know about the girls' birthday. Did you plan something special?"

He grasped his coffee cup and chuckled while a guilty look grew on his face. "I mentioned the girls' birthday to keep you here. I wasn't sure I'd tempted you with the coffee and pie. "

"Did you?"

"I really did, and I'm glad."

"You." She gave his arm a playful punch. As his coffee sloshed onto his pants, she jumped back. "Mike, I'm so sorry."

He patted the hot spot. "Don't worry about it." He grinned and set the cup on the side table. "What would you like to do for their birthday?"

She shifted on her side, leaning her shoulder against the cushion. "It's up to you, but because it's on a Saturday, let's plan something fun for the afternoon."

"I already did."

"What?"

"It's a surprise." He tapped her nose with his finger. "I've been working on it."

"Working on it?" Her mind skittered with questions, her curiosity rising. A surprise for her, too. That seemed unnecessary. Yet her pulse picked up speed in anticipation.

"You'll see." He put a finger over his lips. "I'm not talking."

"Come on, tell me." She leaned over to tickle him. Instead his expression halted her, as his gaze captured hers. Even though he refused to say a word, his eyes told her he planned to do something much better. She slipped into his arms, his lips touching hers. She could wait to find out about the birthday but not for his kisses.

"Wait until you see what I bought the twins for their birthday." Amy stepped into the kitchen carrying shopping bags.

Her grandmother looked over her shoulder and grinned. "You sound as excited as a kid."

"I can't help it." She dropped the packages on the table. "We only had a half day at school today, so I drove to Saginaw."

"All that way?" Grams shook her head.

She dived into the largest bag. "Look." She pulled out two rectangle boxes and turned them to face her grandmother.

"Dolls. They're darling."

"These are special dolls. They come with books and clothes. I picked up a couple of their outfits for the girls' Christmas gifts." She pointed. "This is Rebecca from 1914, and this one is Molly from 1944. I hope they like them."

Grams chuckled. "Any little girl would." She motioned toward the dining room. "I'm having a birthday lunch for them. I talked with Mike."

"Great." She gazed at the purchases again and slipped them back into the bag. "Better hide these. You never know when the girls will show up to see you."

Grams shook her head. "Me? You're number one in their eyes."

A sweet sensation washed over her as she carried the packages into her room. To safeguard, Amy shoved them into the closet before pulling off her coat. She reached into her pocket and dug out her cell phone, and when she did, a text message appeared on the screen.

She peered at it wondering how she'd missed the beeps. She tossed the cell on the bed and hung her coat on a hook in the closet. After slipping off her shoes, she tucked her feet into her fuzzy slippers, then sank onto the bed. She hit the cell phone button and worked her way to the message.

Her heart plummeted. The assistant superintendent of schools in Chicago. Her hands trembled as she gripped the phone.

Job openings are available in several elementary schools in Chicago. Please contact me ASAP for more details. We want to welcome you back.

Job openings. Chicago. She checked her watch. It was too late to call now. She reread the message, her heart beating through her chest. She sank onto the pillow, tears blurring her eyes. This is what she'd waited to hear, and now that her wish had been answered, it tore at her heart. Life in Chicago beckoned her. Her friends. Her job. The life she'd known.

But instead of relief, she ached. In the past few days, she'd made a decision, but now the phone call added a new twist. She closed her eyes as her mind wrapped around the laughter of two little girls who'd grown to care about her, and she, them. Mike's strong arms flooded her memory. Them tumbling into the fall leaves. The tree-lighting and his singing. The hayride. The snow angels. The walk in the woods. Their kisses among the pines.

Tears fell, rolling down her cheeks, her mind tugging one way and then the other. She realized that Chicago would always hold a place in her heart.

She squeezed her eyes together and drew in a deep breath. She'd made her decision.

Chapter Eleven

Amy rolled into Mike's garage on the snowmobile with Ivy clinging to her back. She turned off the motor and released her tight grip from the handlebars. As they came to a stop, the girls' giggles delighted her. They'd been so excited when they opened their first gifts, the snowmobile suits and helmets. They didn't ask questions but hurried off to get ready, although Ivy tripped over the suit as she ran. Amy grinned. The birthday surprise had been a success—and a surprise for her, too. But she nearly panicked facing an afternoon on a snowmobile. She'd never driven one before.

Ivy hopped off the sled, and the two girls darted for the house anxious for their other gifts. She couldn't wait to give them the dolls, but the impending issue sent her emotions haywire. She would tell

Mike today about the new job offer, but when? She didn't want to distract from the girls' birthday with her news.

She slipped off Laura's helmet and climbed off, wearing Mike's too-big bib and parka. She looked like the abominable snowman in his gear. When he faced her, he laughed again.

Amy shook her finger. "This wasn't my idea."

He slipped his arm around her back. "Thanks for going along with it. These two sleds have been sitting here since before the girls were born. I started tuning them up a while ago, hoping one day I could use them again with someone."

His admission wended its way to her heart. "I had no idea what I was doing, and I had one of your daughters on the back."

"I knew you'd do great."

They stepped through the garage door, and she walked ahead as he closed it. As she stepped inside, the girls' voices sailed from their bedroom, and she moved into the half bath to slip back into her clothes. Her cheeks burned from the crisp wind, and so did her heart. The confusion she'd faced had ended, and only telling Mike and the girls was left.

When she walked into the kitchen, Mike stood beside the counter. "I'm making coffee, and the girls voted for pizza." He beckoned her to the living room where the girls were seated close to the lighted

Christmas tree, the homemade ornaments warming her heart. Their birthday packages lay next to them.

Mike patted the sofa cushion and Amy sank beside him.

Ivy grasped a box and hugged it. "I love the puzzles Gramma Ellie gave us."

"And the birthday lunch she cooked for us." In the past weeks, Holly's expression had taken on a loving glow. The old determination had taken a backseat.

Mike caught the girls' attention. "I meant to tell you both how happy I was that you thanked her for the gifts and the lunch. It made me proud."

They beamed, although their focus stayed on the gifts.

When Mike gave the go-ahead, they tore into their presents—a game, new hair ribbons and new clothes for school. When they ripped off the paper of Amy's gift, their eyes widened as they delved into the boxes, pulling out the dolls dressed in their period clothing and the book that told their story.

Holly cuddled the doll to her chest. "I love her."

Amy's eyes moistened as Ivy ran to her, with Molly in one arm, and threw the other around her neck. She planted a kiss on Amy's cheek as love flooded her. "I'm so glad you like them."

"I have one more gift for you." Mike rose and slipped the final package into each girl's lap.

Amy held her breath, knowing they were the picture frames.

When the girls opened the boxes, they lifted their heads, their faces full of awe and their voices mingled. "It's me and Mom."

"It's our mom and us."

The girls exchanged photos, and when Ivy retrieved hers, she sought Mike. "Now we can remember Mom."

Amy's heart tugged.

"I have lots of other pictures for you to look at, too, but those are your very own." Mike had trouble keeping his emotions at bay.

Amy leaned back, not wanting to break the spell. But when the girls settled back again to survey all their birthday gifts, Amy drew in a long breath, sensing this was the best time to tell them. "I have something I wanted to tell you."

Mike's head pivoted as the girls' attention shot to her. A quizzical look grew on Mike's face as she began.

"I received a text message from Chicago. I don't have the details yet, but they have elementary school openings, and they've offered me a job."

The girls' smiles faded as Mike's face paled. "What will you do?"

Her heart beat faster. "I've decided to refuse the offer and accept the one here in Harrisville."

Ivy and Holly's squeal pierced her ears.

Mike drew her into his arms. "You scared me."

"Mike, I wanted you to know I didn't choose Harrisville by default. I chose it because it's where I should be." Her pulse surged as she looked into his eyes. "With you and the girls."

"I'm…ecstatic." He held her close, shaking his head. "But don't scare me like that again."

"Not us either." Holly shook her finger and made Amy laugh.

"Understand?" Ivy's two-sided pigtails bounced as she mimicked her sister's finger shake.

"I promise I won't ever do it again."

A grin grew on Mike's face. "Is it time for Amy's surprise?"

As if jerked by a string, the girls' cry pierced the air. "Yes!" They bounded to his side, their eyes darting from her to their dad and back.

"What surprise?"

He headed for the tree, retrieving a package. "This is for you."

She looked at the silver gift wrap. "Why do I get an early Christmas gift?" She lifted her gaze to his, trying to understand.

Mike held out the package. "It's not a Christmas gift."

Curiosity grew as she studied the gift. "It's not?"

"Open it," Ivy commanded.

Finally it struck her. The girls had made her something special. She pulled the wrap from the box and lifted the lid. Her heart stopped.

"Amy." A faint tremor sounded in Mike's voice. "You told me you were staying, and I talked with the girls, and…"

She gazed at the lovely gold ring. Between the circle of diamonds she read the word *joy*. Her eyes blurred as tears trickled down her cheeks. God had made her path known, and He'd filled her with joy in His presence and in the presence of the three people she loved. When she looked up, she saw tears in Mike's eyes.

"Do you like it?" Ivy's soft voice brushed past her.

She smiled at the girls and gazed into Mike's eyes. "I love it. It's the most wonderful present I've ever received."

"Really?" Holly nestled beside her. "Because we love you."

She captured the sob that broke to her throat. "I love you all so much."

Mike drew her closer. "I thought you might think it too early for an engagement ring, but I hoped that this ring would let you know I love you with all my heart, and when you're ready, I want you to be my wife."

She gazed into his eyes, knowing that time meant nothing when the Lord's hand created the moment. "I'm so ready."

He brushed a kiss across her lips and whispered, "More kisses later."

"Later and forever."

"Forever." Ivy swung around and hugged Holly. "It's not just us anymore."

Holly looked into her sister's eyes. "Now we're a real family."

Amy gazed at the girls' loving embrace, cheeks together as they gazed at her. Their faces shone as bright as the Christmas lights. Amy knelt and drew them into her arms. Could love be any greater? She didn't think so.

Amy sat in the church pew next to Grams, waiting for the children's choir to perform. Mike had sneaked out moments earlier, which surprised her because he was as thrilled to see the girls in the choir as she was.

The sermon ended and a prayer followed. As the ushers passed out small candles to everyone, the piano began to play, and when she looked up, she gasped. Mike stood in front of the Christmas tree, his guitar strapped over his shoulder. He began to play, and his amazing voice filled the church as the words to "Love Has Come" wrapped around her heart.

Grams leaned closer. "Look what God has done."

Struggling with a sob, she could only nod. The words filled her heart. God had given love to the world with the birth of His Son, and He'd also given her love with the gift of a family. The music captivated her, and Mike's gift of music assured her that he had healed from the past as she had finally done.

The ushers returned, lighting candles at the end of the rows. As the flame was passed to each candle, the children's choir filed in. Her chest expanded seeing Ivy and Holly attired in their red Christmas dresses with their hair hanging in the soft curls she'd fashioned for them. They stood side by side like two angels.

Finished with his song, Mike slipped back into his seat and drew Amy's hand into his. The ring he'd given her adorned her finger just as he adorned her life. She whispered, "I love you," and later she would tell him how amazed and proud she'd been to hear him sing.

"Silent Night" began and the children's sweet voices swelled in song as the congregation rose with their lighted candles. The overhead lights dimmed, and the flicker of the candles reflected the glow in her heart.

All is calm. All is bright. The words washed over her, reflecting her new life in Harrisville. She'd finally come home—full and complete.

And loved.

* * * * *

Dear Reader,

The wonder of Christmas captures everyone—children and adults. Families enjoy their special holiday traditions, yet for some, traditions fade as they did for Mike following his wife's death. The death of loved ones seems harder to bear at Christmas. Yet we rejoice because we know they are waiting for us one day. And as Mike said to the twins, love is endless, and even though he and the girls had lost a wife and mother, love opens doors again to new experiences and new relationships. Amy opened a door for Mike and his girls. God hears our prayers and knows our hearts. He provides not only at Christmas, but also every day of our lives.

I hope you enjoyed meeting Amy, Mike, Grams and the twins, who learned to show their love again. I also hope you enjoyed the people of Harrisville, a real small town in northern Michigan.

May your Christmas be blessed, and may you allow the Lord to open doors of love and hope for you this Christmas and always.

Gail Gaymer Martin

Questions for Discussion

1. Amy was set against living in a small town. What changed her mind? What are your impressions of small town living?

2. Christmas is a special time of year filled with traditions and special activities. What traditions do you enjoy at Christmas?

3. Siblings don't always get along, and the twins exemplified this in the book. Why do you think they misbehaved? What changed their behavior?

4. Amy provided some good tips on discipline techniques and she also seemed to understand the reasons these things happen. Discuss her discipline ideas.

5. Although Mike struggled with the twins' discipline, what other good qualities did he have as a father?

6. Have you ever experienced an "old-fashioned" Christmas? What kinds of things did you do to make that Christmas different and special?

7. Grams's faith was strong, and even though Amy

was a believer, hers seemed weak. What kinds of things can weaken someone's faith? And what keeps faith strong?

HER CHRISTMAS COWBOY

Brenda Minton

To my editor, Melissa Endlich.

For God so loved the world that He gave His only begotten son, that whosoever believeth in Him should not perish but have everlasting life.

—*John* 3:16

Chapter One

If life had been fair, Elizabeth Harden would have been on a beach in the Caribbean. Instead she was knee-deep in cow manure. Okay, not exactly knee-deep, but she was standing backstage at a charity bull riding event in Tulsa, Oklahoma, that her dad should have attended had things gone the way they were meant to.

She stepped to the side as a herd of bull riders walked past. Her back pushed against a metal gate and her heel caught on a power cord. She moved to the left and the action was followed by the cameraman. He moved with her, keeping the offending black camera close. She blinked and turned away from the bright light.

Two more hours and she'd be on a jet heading back to St. Louis. She could handle this for two more hours. She could handle the crowds of people. The cheering. The smiles. She could handle hiding the fact that she was falling apart on the inside.

At least for the next hour or so she could think about something other than her lonely apartment, the wedding gifts waiting to be returned, the ring she'd put back in the box after Richard's phone call a week before their wedding and the dress hanging in her mother's bathroom.

For the next hour she could focus on the children this charity event would help. She could get her head on straight and remember that being jilted was nothing compared to children living in poverty. This event had been organized by her dad and a few other men to provide food and gifts for those children.

So she smiled at the cameraman, his infernally bright light and the reporter who wanted to ask a few questions during intermission.

"I'm sorry, we'll get this done." The reporter stepped with her as they tried to stay out of the way in the crowded aisle, surrounded by bulls, cowboys and sponsors.

"It's okay." What else did she have to do?

Another small group of men pushed past. One of the cowboys in the group, tall and lanky with wavy light brown hair and black-framed glasses shot her a grin. Elizabeth didn't smile back. Smiling took too much effort. Instead she glanced away, giving her attention back to the reporter who wanted to know why Harden Industries had become interested in bucking bulls.

She had no idea why other than the fact that her

dad loved a new challenge. Last year it had been NASCAR. This year he'd invested in bucking bulls owned by a rancher named Tim Cooper. Elizabeth filled in a few details for the reporter, trying to remember everything her dad had told her as he packed his suitcase the previous weekend.

"So why are you here rather than your father?" the reporter, a smiling woman in jeans and a Western shirt, asked.

Elizabeth let out a sigh. Behind her bulls bellowed in temporary pens that had been set up that afternoon. She'd watched as panels were set up and loads of dirt brought in to cover the floor, transforming a college basketball stadium into a rodeo arena.

Why *wasn't* Frank Harden here to represent his company? Why had he sent his assistant, his daughter? Because Elizabeth's parents were on her honeymoon? She pasted on a happy smile and told the easy answer, "My parents are on vacation."

The smile got tight and her eyes watered. The reporter gave her a sympathetic smile and touched her arm.

"Thanks, Ms. Harden, I appreciate the interview. If you'd like to join us on the catwalk, you can."

The catwalk was a metal bridge that ran behind the chutes where bulls were being penned for the rides. She'd rather not. She'd prefer to go home now. She'd like to hide away somewhere, a place where no one could give her sympathetic looks, where there would be no questions.

Maybe she should have gone on her honeymoon. Alone. She could have spent Christmas sitting on the beach, the way she'd been planning for months. Only in her plans, she hadn't been alone.

Her heart ached again. It was an odd ache, part anger, part betrayal and sadness. She hadn't wanted to admit, still wouldn't put a name on the other ingredient mixed in with the heartache. She felt too guilty to even think about it.

"I think I'll grab a soda and join you later." She excused herself, touching the reporter's arm and ready to make her escape.

"You'll enjoy it. Just give it a chance." The reporter, Janice, smiled again. She was genuinely nice. "But ignore Travis Cooper. He's a heartbreaker."

"Travis Cooper?"

"Tim Cooper's son. He was the cute guy flirting as he walked past. He's not a rider, he's a bullfighter."

"Bullfighter?"

The reporter laughed a little. "You really are new to this."

"I'd much rather be at the ballet."

"Think of it as a dance, bull against rider. The bullfighters are the guys that put their lives on the line for the riders. Watch in the arena, the three guys that are there to jump between the bull and the rider as he hops off, they're bullfighters."

Over the tall, metal pipe panels that made up the arena, she could see the action. Intermission was over. A rider was spinning out of the chute on the back of a bull. One amazing twist and the cowboy on the back of the bull went flying. A bullfighter, dressed in bright blue and yellow, jumped forward and grabbed the fallen rider by the back of the shirt, quickly tossing him out of danger and then taking a near hit to his own backside.

"They're fearless," the reporter said with serious appreciation.

"I'm sure they are." Elizabeth managed a grim smile. "See you later."

She turned and walked down the narrow aisle, past the temporary bull pens and cowboys standing in small groups. A bull bellowed and crashed against his pen. Another bull joined the ruckus. Elizabeth glanced back and watched the animals moving around in the pens. The bull from the last ride ran out of the arena and through the narrow aisle intended to get him back to the pens. From the other side of the fence she watched the big animal trot past and she was glad for that fence that separated them.

As she walked away from the action a shout went up. She turned, frozen as a bull clambered against pens. She shivered and hurried toward the exit. Another shout went up, louder, more excited. She kept walking.

Metal crashed and men called to each other. Elizabeth started to turn and before she could, a hard body hit her from the side. Strong hands lifted her from the ground and she flew over the gate to her left. Before she could gather herself, a body landed next to hers.

On the other side of the panel a blur of gray, hooves pounding and then a rider on horseback and a length of rope flying through the air.

"Well, that was close." Her rescuer sat next to her, long legs clad in blue shorts stretched in front of him. He wore cleats, not boots. His hat was askew and those dark-framed glasses tilted awkwardly on his nose.

"What happened?" She shivered and a chill ran up her spine and down her arms.

He stood and reached for her hand to pull her up. "I think I saved your life, city girl."

"I think you nearly broke my neck."

"Is that how you talk to your knight in shining cleats?"

She shivered again, thinking about that bull pounding past them. The bull she could have been in front of had he not thrown her over the fence.

"Thank you." She was on her feet, standing next to him. His smile flirted and flashed dimples. "By the way, I'm Elizabeth Harden."

He took off his hat and swept a deep bow in front of her. "My pleasure, ma'am. Travis Cooper, at your service."

He had an accent, not the Southern one he tried to affect. She knew that the Coopers had several adopted children. She guessed that he must be one of them.

When he stood back up, he grimaced. The smile and dimples dissolved.

"Did the bull get you?"

He stretched, raising his arms over his head and twisting. Next he pushed his chin right, then left. His neck cracked and snapped. She cringed. He smiled again.

"Nah, just pulled a muscle jumping over the panel." He put a foot on the bottom rail of the panel. "You okay?"

"I'm fine. Thank you. You didn't tell me what happened." She couldn't look away because his blue-green eyes flashed with laughter, holding her attention. "Other than the part where you saved my life."

He scaled the fence and hopped to the other side. His confident grin probably worked on most women, she guessed. The glasses gave him an almost studious look. "A bull managed to push a panel loose and get out."

"Does that happen often?"

"Almost never. To make it up to you, I could buy you a late dinner."

"No, thank you, I'm flying out as soon as this is over."

He shrugged as if it really didn't matter one way or the other. "Suit yourself."

A tip of his bent-up cowboy hat and he was gone. And her legs felt like a cross between jelly and spaghetti. Of course it was adrenaline that caused the reaction. It definitely had nothing to do with an overly confident cowboy with a smile that melted a girl's insides. Not hers, of course. She was immune, thanks to Richard.

After he walked away she found a seat at the edge of the arena. The rows around her were filled with kids from the group home that would receive a large portion of the proceeds from the event. The kids wore T-shirts and jeans. A few wore shiny, new boots. The little girl sitting next to Elizabeth smiled a gap-toothed smile.

"Is this your first bull ride event?" Elizabeth smiled at the little girl, faded jeans and a T-shirt with a picture of the cowboy who had saved her from the bull. A straw hat was pushed down on the child's wheat-colored hair.

The child nodded and held on to a poster of one of the bull riders. Her attention focused on the arena. Elizabeth took the hint and let her gaze drop to the arena, the chutes and the cowboys.

Her gaze landed on her rescuer. She smiled, remembering his description of himself. Her knight in cleats. He stood to one side, facing the chute that was about to open. As if he felt her watching, he turned and dipped a courtly bow. Her heart tugged a little. The child sitting next to her giggled. Elizabeth smiled at her, at the dimples and sunshine in a face scrubbed clean.

The gate to the chute opened and the bullfighter hurried forward. A rider ripped from the chutes on the back of a black bull that twisted, bucked and went airborne trying to put the cowboy on the ground.

Travis Cooper jumped in front of the bull as the buzzer sounded eight seconds and the rider leaped.

Travis knew that being distracted was a bad, bad thing for a bullfighter. He needed to be focused on the bull, on the guy riding the bull, and not the pretty redhead watching him from the side of the arena.

He shot her one more look and then took a wild leap forward because JP Garret wasn't so lucky tonight. His hand was hung up in the bull rope and he was bouncing against the side of that old angus bull like a ragdoll hanging from a car window.

"Stay loose, JP." Travis jumped as the bull ran past, leaping for the bull and the rope that held JP to the side of the animal. The rosin on the rope kept it tight around the cowboy's hand. JP hopped alongside the bull, trying to stay on his feet and trying to keep up with the raging animal.

Adrenaline rushed through Travis's veins, sending his heart on a crazy race as he jumped at the bull rope a second time, trying to pull it loose. JP must have twisted a few times on his way off to keep that rope this tight on his gloved hand.

One of the other bullfighters grabbed at the bull to slow down his wild, bucking run. Travis pulled and the rope came loose. John McKnight, the third man on their team, grabbed JP and flung him away from the bull as the rope came loose. Travis jumped back.

The crazy bull wasn't done playing. The animal turned, brought his head low and then flung up, flinging slobber while catching Travis under the jaw and sending him flying.

Travis rolled and his brain jarred as he hit the ground. The crowd was a buzz in the background. It took a minute for the world to settle. A medic reached him as he got to his feet.

"Travis, you okay?"

The guy's face blurred. Travis shook his head to clear his addled brain. "Yeah, I'm good."

"Can you tell me where you are?"

Travis blinked and adjusted his glasses. He found the person he sought. She sat on the second row and she clearly wasn't enjoying herself.

"Travis?"

"I'm in Tulsa, and if it was a good night, I'd be sitting next to her." He nodded in the direction of Elizabeth Harden.

"Yeah, well, you're talking to me instead." The medic smiled and slapped Travis on the back.

Travis cringed at the skull-jarring blow. "I'm good."

"Yeah, but have the doc check you out later."

"Will do." Travis pushed his hat down on his head and saluted the other two bullfighters. "Just a hard day at the office, guys."

Chuck Collins laughed. "Ain't that the truth. And someone just said that the rain is starting to freeze. Looks like a good night to be driving home."

Travis shook his head and regretted the action that sent a sharp pain down his head and into his neck. He pushed his hat on a little tighter. Freezing rain and a trailer load of bulls. Not exactly what he'd call a good night.

As the next rider slid onto the bull in the chute, Travis glanced to the left and watched as Elizabeth Harden got up and walked out of the stands. Her hand brushed at her cheeks.

He'd heard she'd gotten jilted. Frank Harden shared the news. What kind of man didn't walk her down the aisle and make her his wife? Yeah, he knew what that guy needed. But he didn't have time to let his imagination run wild, thinking about what should happen to the guy that walked out on her. The gate opened and the bull exploded from the confines of the chute. The first jump nearly unseated the rider.

Travis stayed close to the spinning, one-ton animal. His head ached and his eyes blurred. Over the crowd and the thunder of hooves on packed dirt, he could hear the ping of ice on the roof of the stadium.

The rider made it to the buzzer. Travis tossed his hat at the head of the bull to distract the animal and give the guy a good chance at a clean getaway.

As the bull ran out of the arena, Travis glanced up. He saw his mom on the catwalk talking to their new partner. Actually, she was the daughter of their new partner. Frank Harden had wanted to invest in one of the fastest-growing sports. Tim Cooper, Travis's dad, eagerly accepted a partner with the money to build up their business.

That didn't concern Travis as much as the scene

unfolding in front of him. Why in the world did Travis's mom have that look on her face, the one that clearly spelled big trouble for him? As if on cue, she looked his way and smiled. Her arm was around Elizabeth's waist. The two were talking. Not good at all.

And then the arena's lights went out and none of it mattered. Nothing like a freak ice storm in mid-December to really stir things up. He didn't even have a flashlight. Surely they had generators in a venue this size. He waited. Nothing happened. Great. He loved the dark. He just hoped they'd gotten that last bull in the pen and it wasn't lurking in the arena about to charge him from behind. Or from the front. Or even the side.

Elizabeth stood on the metal catwalk, bulls beneath her, cowboys all around her and total darkness holding everything at a standstill. She didn't want to move because she didn't know if she'd fall off the bridge into a pen full of bulls.

"Well, this never happens." Angie Cooper stood next to her.

"I bet it doesn't." Elizabeth tried to force lightness to her tone. "What should we do?"

"Hang tight. They'll get the power back on in a minute."

"I wonder how bad the roads are."

Angie leaned close. "Probably bad enough that planes won't be flying out. Don't worry, we won't leave you stranded here alone."

"I'll be fine. If the flight doesn't take off tonight, I can fly out tomorrow."

"Nevertheless, I wouldn't dream of leaving until we know what you'll be doing. No one wants to be alone at this time of year."

"I'm used to it." She hadn't meant to sound pitiful, just that she was used to taking care of herself. She traveled quite often for Harden Industries. "Really, I have a lot to take care of back home. I'll get the first available flight."

In the dark she couldn't see Angie Cooper's face, or any looks of disbelief. What did Elizabeth have to rush home to? An empty apartment? No plans for the holidays? She had no brothers or sisters to turn to. She didn't have cousins, aunts or uncles in the area.

Christmas had never been a big family holiday for the Hardens. They'd always gotten away for the holidays. Christmas meant somewhere warm, a beachfront condo or a house in Jamaica, not snowmen and caroling. Her parents put up a tree as a part of holiday party decor, not to celebrate the season.

"We can't let Frank Harden's daughter sit in a hotel room by herself, not with Christmas just around the corner."

"But I'm fine. Really. I can do some shopping. Or…"

In the darkened building an arm went around her shoulders and Angie leaned close. "It won't hurt forever."

Elizabeth closed her eyes and said a silent thank-you for the dark that kept anyone from seeing the tears that slid down her cheeks. Her throat tightened and she nodded. Angie Cooper hugged her closer.

And then the lights flashed on.

Travis Cooper stood in the arena, twenty feet away. Elizabeth locked gazes with the cowboy in bright blue-and-yellow shorts, a bent cowboy hat shoved down on light brown, almost blond hair. He touched the brim of his hat and winked.

A loud voice on the PA system announced that the event was being cancelled. The crowd broke into a buzz of conversation. People started moving from their seats. Cowboys pulled off gloves, talked to each other and disbanded.

Angie kept a hand on Elizabeth's arm. "Let's see what the men are doing. We'll find out more about the weather situation."

As they maneuvered through the exiting crowds, a hand touched Elizabeth's back and someone moved close. She glanced up to the man on her left side.

"This way. Dad and the guys are loading bulls." Travis Cooper slipped around Elizabeth and walked close to his mother, blocking her from the crowds of people pushing around them.

"How are the roads?" Angie Cooper kept Elizabeth close.

"Not too bad if we take it slow." Travis kept them moving forward. "But the airport is already starting to cancel flights. You might need to change your travel plans."

"I can get a room near the airport so I'm close by when they reopen."

"How are you going to get there?" he asked.

"A taxi?"

Travis Cooper shook his head. "Not tonight, not out here."

"Travis can take you." Angie Cooper gave her son a look. "We aren't going to leave her stranded. She can come home with us, or you can take her to the hotel."

"Of course, I'll drive you wherever you need to go. I have to stay in town anyway." Travis eased them through the crowd and Elizabeth thought of a dozen ways to regain the control that was quickly slipping from her grasp.

She had an idea that Travis Cooper felt the same way.

Chapter Two

Travis guided his mom and Elizabeth Harden through the crowds. People lined the walls, waiting for their rides. One of the models representing a local boat dealer smiled and winked as he walked past. She'd slipped him her number earlier. He'd already lost it.

His mom shook her head and heat climbed into his cheeks at the warning. Yeah, he knew what that look meant. He liked women. Beautiful women, funny women, serious women. He hadn't met one who he didn't find interesting. He hadn't met one who had ever given him the slightest itch to settle down.

He wasn't planning on calling the model. She was pretty, but he wasn't interested.

"Did you bring luggage?" he asked Elizabeth as they hurried down a quiet hallway to an exit the stock contractors used.

"No, I hadn't planned on staying."

His mom patted her back. "Come home with us. We'll let this storm pass and then reschedule your flight."

Travis drew in a deep breath, experiencing a catch in his ribs that he hadn't noticed while the adrenaline had been pumping. He made pretty serious eye contact with his mom. Yeah, he knew what she was all about. She wanted to fix Elizabeth Harden. He doubted the woman in question really wanted to be fixed right now.

"You don't have to drive me. I'm sure I can get a taxi." She glanced back, smiling as she gave him an out.

Travis liked that she was trying to make her escape in a sweet way, so as not to hurt his mom. Angie Cooper meant well. She was a fixer, an encourager and a real serious matchmaker.

"It isn't any trouble." Travis pushed the door open. His dad's truck and the trailer were nearby, idling in the cold night, exhaust plumes thick in the chilly air. Ice pinged against the vehicles, against the ground, against the metal roof.

"I can't believe this weather." Elizabeth shrugged into a coat that wasn't meant for a serious slice of arctic air.

"So much for the 'slight chance' forecast," Travis grumbled as he fished keys from his pocket. "I have meetings here tomorrow, with the Samaritans' Group Home. Hopefully we won't have to cancel."

The bull riding event had been for the group home. The money they raised would help buy Christmas gifts, clothes and other needed items for a home that housed about twenty kids.

His mom slid on the ice. He grabbed her arm and held her tight. He reached for Elizabeth as she started to slide, pulling her close. "Hold on, ladies."

They reached the truck and his dad opened the door for his mom, helping her up. "I warmed your truck up with my key."

Travis nodded. He still had hold of Elizabeth Harden and he was having a difficult time focusing. Her coat was soft suede, all fashion and no sense. "Right. Thanks, Dad."

"No problem. You're staying in town?" Tim Cooper glanced from Elizabeth to Travis.

"I am. I have a few things to take care of. You sure you want to tackle these roads tonight?" Travis answered, and he just wanted out of the cold.

Tim nodded. "Yeah, I don't think it's as bad toward home. I called Jackson and he said it hasn't started to freeze on the roads, just the fences and trees."

"Jackson answered his phone?"

Tim nodded and his attention refocused on Elizabeth. "You're more than welcome to come on out to the ranch."

"No, I should stay in town and wait for the airport to reopen."

"Travis will take you to a good hotel and make

sure you're settled." Tim, always old-school, tipped his hat before turning his attention back to Travis. "Take care of yourself and don't get in a hurry."

"Will do, Dad." Travis stepped away from his dad, a hand on the woman still at his side. His cleats slid a little but he managed to get traction.

"I can't believe this is happening." Elizabeth leaned close. He considered taking off his coat and tossing it over her shoulders. But he thought she was the type of woman who wouldn't appreciate a whole lot of chivalry. Instead he concentrated on making it to the truck without getting all tangled up and falling on the pavement.

When they reached his truck, he jerked the door open. It had already started to freeze. Ice covered the handle and coated the paint. "Easy getting in."

"No problem." She climbed in. He stood in the open door, waiting. "Will we be able to get to the hotel?"

"Oh, sure we will. Okay, maybe not the one closest to the airport, but we'll get somewhere. They might have rooms at the place where I'm staying."

"Thank you. I wasn't prepared for this."

"Yeah, you never know what's going to happen." He pulled the seat belt and handed it to her. "Life's funny that way."

She froze, staring at him. The arctic air swirled and his mind lost track of what he'd been thinking or why he'd said what he'd said. She'd been jilted a week before her wedding. He had one word for a guy that would do that. Or maybe a few choice words. *Loser* would do.

What kind of man was this guy and why in the world would she have wanted to marry him? Travis shook his head. "Buckle up."

He closed the truck door and eased himself around to the driver's side. Man, the ice was coming down hard. He didn't like this. He didn't like it one bit.

"Are we going to make it?" Elizabeth peered out the windshield at the glistening, ice-covered roads. The windshield wipers scraped and squeaked as they pushed against the frozen precipitation. Christmas lights hanging on electric poles glistened and wavered through the icy windows of the truck.

"Of course we will." But he didn't turn to give her one of his cute little smiles. Instead he leaned closer to the steering wheel and stared straight ahead at the frozen pavement.

The radio didn't play music; instead it was a running account of roads being closed, flights being canceled and streets blocked by accidents.

Elizabeth shivered in the cool interior of the truck. The heater was just starting to blow warm.

"I shouldn't have been here." She sighed as the words slipped out. The last thing she wanted was to get emotional.

"There are worse places to be." Travis didn't turn to look at her but kept his eyes on the road. "I mean, if I had to choose somewhere to be stuck, I'd pick Oklahoma. Especially at Christmas. If you can't fly out, you can always spend some time at Cooper Creek. My parents love company at Christmas."

"I'm glad you feel that way. But they're your family. I'm a stranger."

"I was a stranger when they adopted me. I was five. I didn't speak English. It was about this time of year."

She gave him a careful look, saw him as that little boy coming to a strange land, to have a family made up of strangers. His story was easier to focus on than her own.

"Was it frightening, to be so young, to be taken from everything familiar?"

The truck eased to a stop at a red light, sliding just a little to the right. Travis glanced her way, a quick look before returning his attention back to the road. "Yeah, it was scary. I'd lived in the orphanage in Russia for several years. I knew the workers and children. It wasn't perfect, but it was my home."

"But you wanted to be adopted, didn't you?"

He laughed. "Yeah, I wanted to be adopted. I wanted a family. And the Coopers, they're my family. I wasn't an easy kid."

"No?"

He didn't answer the unasked question. How had he not been easy? He obviously adored his mother. He loved his dad. How had his life been difficult? She wanted to think about anything but her own life.

"Are you hungry?"

Elizabeth shook her head. "Not really. I had nachos at the bull ride."

"That's always a great meal." His smile teased. "I'm sure we can find something to eat, though."

"No, really, I just want to get a room and wait this out."

Alone.

The truck slid. Elizabeth swallowed a screech and held tight to the door. The truck straightened, stayed on the road, and they continued on.

"See how good I am?" Travis winked. "You should trust me."

"I'll remember that." She held back a sigh and watched out the window. City lights glistened in the night. A utility truck drove past them, dumping salt or sand on the frozen street.

"Do you have brothers or sisters?" Travis asked the question after several minutes of silence. Elizabeth glanced away from the window. He was tapping the steering wheel and he looked her way, smiling.

"No."

He laughed and reached to turn up the radio. "I can't imagine being an only child. There are twelve of us, you know. Sometimes an extra kid shows up for a week or two, now that we're all grown. Mom can't handle a quiet house."

"Extra kid?"

"She isn't a full-time foster parent, but she provides respite care for foster parents who need a break or for children who need a temporary home until a permanent placement is found."

"Gotcha." She couldn't imagine a house full of kids. "It's always just been my parents and me. There are a few relatives on either coast that we rarely see."

"When you leave—" he paused, focusing on the road and the ice-covered bridge they were crossing "—what will you do for Christmas?"

In the dark she shrugged, even though he couldn't see. But he also couldn't see the tear that slid down her cheek. She was so done with crying. "Eat out. Maybe go to a movie."

"That's a little pathetic, don't you think?" His accent made the words sound a little funnier than they were meant to be.

Elizabeth smiled. "Yeah, it's pathetic."

"Doesn't that mean he wins?"

Richard, always the winner. And she was the loser who got left for a pretty girl who worked at the perfume counter where he'd bought her a birthday present last summer. She sighed and didn't answer Travis Cooper's question.

He wasn't the person she wanted to have this discussion with. He was filling silence. He was the kind of guy who would fall in love with the girl at the perfume counter, and the next week fall in love with someone new. She'd met his kind, been engaged to his kind.

She had also learned that she couldn't change a guy like him. A zebra didn't change his stripes.

"I'm sorry about that."

His apology came a few minutes later, followed by a cough.

"I mean, it isn't any of my business. But he's a loser for what he did. I don't know the details, so maybe…"

Elizabeth laughed. "So maybe he had a good reason for leaving me?"

He cleared his throat. "No, that isn't what I mean. I mean…"

She peered at him in the dark interior of the truck, lit only by the soft green glow of the dashboard. Ice continued to pelt the windshield and the road. Travis had both hands on the wheel and he shot her a quick look.

"I'm joking." She let him off the hook.

"I know. I'm trying to be a nice guy and say the right things."

"It's all been said. And it isn't as if there's a card for a moment like this."

"I guess it would say something like, 'Congratulations, you escaped marriage to a big loser.'" He didn't laugh, but she did.

"I hadn't thought about it being a congratulations card. I thought it would be a sympathy card."

"Why?" He grinned, his profile strong and a dimple creased his cheek. "Wouldn't you be glad you found out before you married him?"

She let out a pent-up breath and nodded her head.

"Glad hasn't been the exact emotion I've been dealing with."

"No, I guess not." He slowed as the road became more treacherous. "I'm sorry, I should stop talking."

"I do think the card idea is a good one."

He laughed. "Well, sometimes I surprise myself. And here we are, the sweetest hotel in Tulsa."

It was a large Victorian mansion surrounded by tall fences. Lights glistened in the windows and trees were illuminated with sparkling Christmas lights. She'd expected something else, but what did she know about him or the type of hotel he'd pick?

He stopped the truck under a long carport.

"This is a hotel?"

"Yeah, it's a renovated home built at the turn of the century. It's quiet, not a lot of noise and commotion."

"It looks nice." She pushed her door open and stepped out, immediately sliding and having to grab the side of the truck to steady herself.

Travis joined her. "They'll have something to eat, too."

They slid, arm in arm, across the icy driveway. Elizabeth told herself to let go and not get attached to a man who made her smile, feel less broken. But it felt good to laugh again. It was an easy night of not thinking, of letting go. And tomorrow he'd be gone from her life. It was that simple. Maybe that made it easier to smile with him.

"Hold on, this will be treacherous." Travis steadied her as they reached stone steps that took them to the next elevation of the sidewalk.

"I'm good now. You don't have to hold on to me." She reached for the metal handrail, slick with ice.

Travis turned. "I forgot something in the truck."

Before she could react, he wavered, his foot slipped and he started to tumble. Elizabeth tried to scream, but the words froze. Her knight in shining cleats was about to be toast. She grabbed at his arm, but he'd caught himself and was standing, holding the handrail.

"Well, that was almost embarrassing." He smiled up at her, his hat askew.

"Are you okay?"

"Yeah, I think I am." He blinked a few times and shook his head.

"Did you pass out?"

"No, not at all. Why would you think that?" He grabbed the handrail and eased himself up, taking the steps a lot more gingerly than she would have imagined.

"Did you hurt yourself?" She stepped next to him, trying to assess just how injured he was.

"Nah, I've been hurt worse than this." He leaned a little and she wrapped an arm around his waist.

They made the long trek up the icy sidewalk, arm in arm as ice continued to fall. It was slow going with a big cowboy leaning against her, favoring his right ankle and acting none too steady on his feet.

The door opened as they made their way up the

steps. A lady stepped out, tall and gorgeous with thick gray hair and ivory skin.

"Travis Cooper," she greeted and then a spurt of Russian flew between the two. The woman smiled and nodded at Elizabeth.

"Yelena, this is Elizabeth Harden. Her father helped fund the event tonight."

"Oh, this is good. Travis loves that group home."

He obviously came here often. She looked up at the fabulous building and then back to the cowboy and tried to match him to this house.

Travis limped into the foyer of the house. Elizabeth followed. He leaned against the wall for a moment and then turned and smiled as if he hadn't nearly hit the pavement.

"Stop looking at me like that. It's the ice. I fell." He winked and stood tall again. "Yelena, tell me you have something wonderful cooking in that kitchen of yours."

Yelena looked at her watch and gave Travis a long look. "I think you know that I always keep something ready. But this late, it'll have to heat up."

"Just a sandwich. Please don't cook." Elizabeth peeked into the high-ceilinged parlor to her right. It was decorated for Christmas, glowing with lights, a tall tree in the corner and a beautiful manger scene spread across the mantel of the fireplace.

"Oh, it's no problem. I have soup and bread. I'll heat it up in minutes." Yelena led them through a maze of rooms to a large kitchen at the back of the house.

"You have a beautiful home." Elizabeth took the seat that was offered and smiled when Yelena sat a cup of tea in front of her.

"It's a good home. We have a wedding chapel in the back and two honeymoon suites. I'm afraid the only room we have for you is one of the honeymoon suites."

"I don't want to put you out." Elizabeth watched Travis slip off his cleated tennis shoe. She stood. "Do you have ice, or a bag of frozen peas?"

Yelena glanced from her pot of soup to Travis. "Yes, of course. The freezer is out that door."

The room Yelena had pointed to held two freezers, two refrigerators and a laundry facility. Elizabeth poked through the freezer and found a small bag of frozen peas.

Travis had pulled a chair out from the table and had his foot up. She placed the ice on his already-swelling ankle. He flinched and repositioned the bag.

"Do you think we should go to the emergency room?"

Travis raised one brow and grinned. "Really, you want to drive in this weather? Don't worry, it's just a little sprain."

"It's swollen and turning blue."

Yelena left her stove and stepped over to look. "I think she's right."

"I think I know more about injuries than either of you. If you have some duct tape, Yelena, I'll take care of this when I go to my room."

He had to be joking.

"Seriously, duct tape?"

He wasn't joking. "Yes, duct tape. I'll slip my sock back on and tape it up."

"And what about your head?" She leaned, brushing her fingers against the bruise on his cheek and then touching the bump on the side of his head.

"My head is fine."

"Did he take a hit tonight?" Yelena set a tray on the table. There were two bowls of steaming soup and a plate of bread, thickly sliced and slathered with butter.

"I didn't take a hit." Travis reached for a bowl of soup. "And I didn't come here to be mothered."

"He went down in the arena." Elizabeth watched as he salted his soup. She had already taken a spoonful of hers. It was rich with tomatoes and other vegetables.

"I'm *not* going to the E.R." He lifted the spoon to his mouth. "And now, if the two of you don't mind, I've been dreaming about this soup all night."

Elizabeth couldn't agree more. Travis Cooper could take care of himself. She didn't know why she felt the need to play nurse. But as they ate, she watched for signs that indicated his injuries were more severe than he let on. Unfortunately he caught her staring and winked. Of course he'd misunderstood.

* * *

Travis managed to finish his soup without further medical examinations. He watched the two females sitting across from him. He kept a wary eye on them because he'd had a few too many women in his life badgering, clucking and mothering. That's what happened to a guy when he had five sisters. His brother Brian was the youngest, he got the worst of it, but he'd gotten smart and headed off on a mission trip a few years earlier.

"My regular room, Yelena?" He stood, holding the edge of the table just long enough to get his balance.

He tried hard not to look at Elizabeth Harden, with her warm chocolate eyes and soft smile. He wasn't much for sitting and talking, but she had him almost convinced he could sit and talk to her for hours.

Not that he'd ever had a problem talking. But he'd always had a problem sitting still for very long.

She picked up their bowls and carried them to the sink. Yelena shot him a look and then followed her new guest.

"I can get the dishes. You come with me. I'll show you to your room." Yelena headed them both up the side stairs.

Great, stairs. It was hard to be the tough guy when every step he took shot a knife-sharp pain through his ankle. He made it up, one careful step at a time. When they got to the door of his room, he paused. Elizabeth stood there, looking unsure and a little nervous.

"I'll be right here if you need anything," he assured her, wishing he wasn't the absolute wrong guy to hold her for a minute. She didn't need that. She wouldn't want it. And yet she looked as if she needed to be held.

Since when was he Mr. Sensitive?

"I'm fine. I'll see you in the morning."

"Yeah, we'll figure out how to get you home." He leaned against the door.

"You have appointments to keep in the morning," she said.

"Right, but we can get your flight arranged first."

Her smiled eased over him like cool water. "We'll worry about it tomorrow."

She stepped into a room two doors down. One of Yelena's honeymoon suites. He'd stayed in the room once before. It was a bigger room with a Jacuzzi and light-colored furniture. A chick room. She'd like it. He'd felt big and out of place with all the lace and pastels.

He slipped on his glasses and eased into his room, limping to the nearest chair. He dropped the shoe he'd carried, along with the duct tape Yelena had handed him before he headed up the stairs. After a few minutes of just sitting and letting his mind settle, he pulled a length of tape from the roll and wrapped it around his foot and ankle.

Yeah, that would work. He smiled, thinking about the look Elizabeth Harden had given him when he asked Yelena for duct tape. He leaned back in the chair and closed his eyes, trying hard to ignore other thoughts, most of which centered around the woman two doors down from him.

All day he'd looked forward to getting back to this room and settling in for a good night's sleep. That's what he planned on doing and nothing, not even a pretty redhead, could change that for him. But he didn't have the energy to drag his worthless carcass to the bed. Instead he picked up one of the pretty pillows, shoved it behind his head and settled both legs on the ottoman in front of the chair. His head was spinning. His foot was throbbing.

Yeah, this night hadn't gone the way he'd planned. He'd thrown away the phone number of a woman who would have gladly gone out to dinner with him. Instead he'd saddled himself with a woman who wanted nothing more than a quick flight out of Tulsa.

Worse, he'd taken her to the place he usually escaped to when he needed peace and quiet. His mom would tell him that meant something. At that moment, with his head pounding and his ankle throbbing, it was hard to make sense of his reasons for bringing her here.

He could have taken her to a hotel close to the airport. She would have been out of his hair.

Instead, he couldn't get her off his mind.

Chapter Three

Elizabeth knocked on the door again as she glanced at her watch. It was after eight in the morning. She'd been knocking on Travis's door for five minutes. She didn't want to be worried, but the different scenarios flashing through her mind weren't pretty. What if he'd passed out and hit his head? What if he had a concussion and slipped into a coma?

Her hand trembled on the doorknob. She took a deep breath and turned. It flew open from the inside and he was standing there, freshly shaved, hair still damp and a towel around his shoulders. At least he was fully clothed.

"Breaking and entering, Ms. Harden?"

"No, worried that you were in here comatose, Mr. Cooper."

He winked. "I'm feeling much better this morning. I couldn't get my boots on, but that's why someone invented duct tape. Have you looked out the window?"

"Yes, the whole world is an ice cube. I'm not sure

why that makes you happy." She'd already called the airport. They were hoping flights would resume by late afternoon.

Travis Cooper didn't seem to remember that she needed to go home. Today. Instead he was leaning against the door frame, staring at her through dark-framed glasses and smiling.

"Haven't you ever wondered what heaven looks like? I picture the crystal sea looking a lot like the world covered in ice and then glistening in bright sunlight." He tossed the towel into a chair as he talked.

She'd never thought of crystal seas, or anything else pertaining to heaven, other than to wonder how people could be so sure that God would let them into His perfect creation.

"It is beautiful. Very inconvenient, but beautiful."

"What, you had important plans for today?" He stepped out of the room, one foot in a boot, the other foot wrapped in gray tape.

"Don't you have plans for today? Isn't that why you stayed in Tulsa?"

He shrugged and eased down the stairs, left leg first. "I have a lot of plans, but if it doesn't get done, it isn't the end of the world."

She shook her head at that. "Don't you have business with the group home that has to be dealt with?"

"I'll get it done."

"But..."

"You have a pocket calendar in your purse, don't

you? And a gadget on your phone to let you know what appointments to keep each day?"

She didn't answer.

"I think one appointment we should keep is with the emergency room." She slowed her steps to match his.

"I'm fine. Yelena's husband is a doctor. He'll be around to check on me."

"You know them that well?"

He laughed. "Her husband is my uncle. They immigrated to the states a few years ago and they found me."

"I see. You have more family than you know what to do with."

"I know exactly what to do with family. I keep them close. Unless I need a break."

She guessed he came here for those breaks.

By the time they made it to the dining room, his slow steps were making her cringe. The formal dining room of the bed-and-breakfast had tall windows, several tables and more greenery, plus a large tree in the far corner. Everything was Christmas. She hadn't put up a tree for several years.

Travis sat down. Elizabeth pulled an extra chair close and patted it. "Put your foot up."

"Yes, dear." His smile faded. "I'm sorry."

"No, don't worry about it. I take over. I don't mean to, but in my world I'm used to getting things done."

"I understand. You're a little like my older sister. She's always responsible."

"Don't say it as if it's a bad thing."

He turned toward the door, his smile brightening. "Uncle Uri, good to see you."

A tall man, silver-haired and with wire-framed glasses perched on a straight nose, walked into the room. He smiled and pulled out a chair at the table next to theirs.

"I've seen you several times during the night." Travis's uncle leaned and looked into his eyes. "I woke you up."

"I guess you did."

His uncle studied the duct tape–bandaged ankle. "You think that's going to fix it?"

"I guess it will."

Uri shook his head. "About the ankle, I'll take a look later, without the tape. But I have crutches in the closet. Stay off it and no driving."

"I have a lot to do today. Elizabeth needs a ride to the airport."

Uri stood. "Elizabeth won't have a flight out today. Backlog. I know the rest you aren't going to listen to."

"Probably not, but thanks anyway."

"You're welcome. Yelena has breakfast on the buffet." He nodded to a table covered with a white cloth. Stainless steel warmers lined the table, steam rising from beneath the lids.

Elizabeth had caught the scent of cinnamon when they first entered the room. "I'll get you a plate."

"I can do it." Travis started to stand. His uncle placed a hand on his shoulder.

"You sit."

Travis shook his head. "You all understand that at home I'd be out feeding cattle, probably cleaning stalls."

"And you're not at home, nephew. My home. My rules." Uri didn't smile. "I mean it."

Elizabeth lifted lids from the warming trays. "Do you want biscuits and gravy? Scrambled eggs. Oh, waffles."

"All of the above." He said it with an obvious frown in his tone.

Elizabeth turned. "I'm sorry. Sometimes life is taken out of our hands."

He laughed then. "I think I might have said something like that to you."

"Yes, but I'm the one who likes a schedule. You're the one without a calendar. Right?"

"But today was important. The kids are expecting Santa."

She carried the plate to him and sat it on the table. "Let me guess. You're Santa."

"I'm Santa." He turned a little pink.

She tried to picture him as Santa. The image just didn't work. Santa didn't wear Wranglers and a cowboy hat. Santa didn't tape his ankle with duct tape. Santa was jolly. Travis Cooper was...

She looked away.

"A skinny, cowboy Santa. Sorry, I'm not seeing it."

"Yeah, well, I'm a good Santa."

She went back for her plate. When she returned to the table, she'd made up her mind because the children she'd seen last night deserved to have their Christmas. "I'll drive you to the group home."

He smiled the most delicious smile and she knew she'd made a mistake. "Thank you, Mrs. Claus. But what will the kids think on Christmas Day when you're not there to help deliver the gifts?"

"Oh no, I'm not Mrs. Claus. I'm just an angry elf who missed her flight north."

As she sat down, unfolding her napkin, Travis reached for her hand. Before she could pull back he lifted it, brushing a kiss across the back of her knuckles.

"We've got to see if we can find you some Christmas cheer, Mrs. Claus. Maybe a little joy and some faith."

Elizabeth pulled her hand back to her lap. "Bah humbug, Santa."

"You're not a Scrooge, Elizabeth. You just have to find Christmas."

"Find it?"

He touched his chest. "Yeah, in here. Don't worry, I'll help you."

An hour later Elizabeth wasn't sure she wanted help finding Christmas. Not when it meant driving Travis Cooper's truck on the icy streets of Tulsa, Oklahoma, as he sat in the passenger seat cringing as if someone was throwing knives at him.

"Stop looking so antsy." She slowed at an intersection. The light stayed green, and she eased through.

"Sorry, that's something I can't really change."

She quickly glanced his way because she really didn't want to take her eyes off the road. "Is it my driving? You know, I grew up in St. Louis and we have ice there, too."

"I kind of figured you had a driver."

"I've been working since I was fifteen. My dad believes that hard work builds character. I think he'd take a dim view of having me driven anywhere."

Her father had taught her to work hard, stick to a schedule and make goals. Those lessons had served her well in life. They were lessons Travis Cooper should learn.

"I'm sorry. And you're doing a good job. My knuckles are barely white." He flexed his fingers. "Turn up here to the right. And really, your driving doesn't bother me."

"That's good to know. How are you going to get home?"

She wasn't going to offer. She wasn't going to offer. She repeated the phrase to herself, over and over again, in case she wasn't getting it.

I'll figure something out."

Nope. She wasn't going to offer.

"Do I keep going straight?" She eased on the brake before hitting a long stretch of ice. The truck slid just a little.

"That big brick house at the end of this street." He closed his eyes and leaned back.

"Do you actually dress like Santa?"

Eyes flashed open, blue-green with dark lashes. "Yeah, I dress like Santa. Why is that so hard to believe?"

"I kind of pictured Santa as an older guy."

"Yeah, but you're a Scrooge, so what do you know?"

She pulled into the driveway of the big house and parked close to the front door. Her heart raced and she knew a moment of fear.

"This is way outside of my comfort zone," she admitted.

"What, being Mrs. Claus or the kids?"

"Both, I think. You know, we usually spend Christmas on a beach somewhere." She'd never thought of that as empty. Now it felt pathetically so.

"Sounds like a good time, just lacking Christmas cheer." He opened his door. "Let yourself have fun, Elizabeth."

Right, fun. She met him at the front of the truck. Santa on crutches. A skinny Santa in faded jeans and a plaid shirt under a Carhartt coat. They walked up the front steps together. He hopped, she walked.

At the top of the steps he settled the crutches under his arms again and knocked on the door. It opened and a motherly lady in a blue dress covered with a flour-stained apron opened the door.

"Travis, you're here. We really didn't know if you'd

make it, with the ice and all." She motioned them inside. "And what happened to you?"

"It's a long story. It started with a concussion and ended with icy steps. I've always been graceful."

She laughed and motioned them down the hall in the direction of the sweet scent of cookies. "The kids are in the activity room. Your costume is in the back bathroom."

"That sounds good. Jemma, have you met Mrs. Claus?"

Jemma turned, her eyes widening, her mouth opening in surprise. "Mrs.?"

Travis laughed. "Just for today. No wedding bells for this cowboy. Elizabeth Harden, meet Jemma Coburn. She and her husband, Dutch, run this place."

"With a lot of help." Jemma wiped her hands on her apron and held one out to Elizabeth. "Thank you for supporting our home."

"You're welcome." Elizabeth didn't know what else to say. Harden Industries had helped many charities over the years. But Elizabeth didn't get involved in those activities. Her mom took care of charitable contributions and events.

"Well, let's get this show on the road." Travis pulled off his hat. "Lead the way, Jemma. I think there are kids here who want to see Santa."

Jemma laughed. "Travis, you know that most of them don't believe…"

He put a finger to his mouth. "Shh, you'll break Elizabeth's heart if you say it."

* * *

Travis watched Elizabeth turn three shades of red. Yeah, he was getting back in his groove. He'd always talked too much, but he'd also usually known what to say to a woman. With Elizabeth Harden he seemed to be saying the wrong thing more often than not.

But back at the house, when he'd kissed her hand, that had been a moment. And then he'd felt guilty. She'd been hurt, broken, left. She deserved more than a cowboy who flirted out of habit.

She deserved to smile, not look like a scared rabbit. That's how she looked as Jemma led them down the hall to the bathroom where the costumes were being kept.

As she walked close to his side, he noticed something else, something he'd already noticed in the very long truck ride from Yelena and Uri's to Samaritan House. Elizabeth Harden smelled like spring and warm sunshine.

"We'll let Elizabeth go first." Jemma reached into a closet and pulled out a red dress, black boots and a cap. "Mrs. Claus, your wardrobe."

Elizabeth took the costume, held it out and looked at it.

"I thought you were kidding." She shot him a look and he shrugged it off.

"I never tease." He winked and she laughed just enough to let him know she'd survive this.

"Fine, but you really owe me."

"You're keeping a list?" He took the Santa costume that Jemma handed him.

"I am definitely keeping a list." She stepped into the bathroom, closing the door behind her.

She walked out and for a few minutes he believed in Santa. Especially if she was really Mrs. Claus. The dress was loose, but she'd tightened a belt around the waist. The boots were clunky and scuffed. But wow, she wasn't the type of woman a man cheated on or left at the altar.

She was forever, wrapped up with a bow. And he was the last person who should be having thoughts like that. He was the guy who considered three dates a long-term relationship.

"Okay, I'm going to get dressed." He eased past her, distracted and nearly tripping over the metal crutches.

"Don't fall."

"Never." He would never fall. He'd never fallen before. But he was pretty close, he decided. If this was what falling felt like, he just hoped that someone like her was on the other end to catch him.

When he walked out of the bathroom, she laughed. He stood there, feeling kind of ridiculous in the red pants and jacket made of red velvet and trimmed with white fluff. The boots were big and the right boot fit over his swollen, taped ankle. He leaned on the crutches, knowing why she was laughing. He had kept his hat in favor of the Santa hat that had come with the costume. The white fake beard drooped low on his chin.

"Well, aren't you a jolly old soul." Elizabeth in the red velvet dress had the nerve to make fun of him. He drew close to her.

"I wouldn't laugh if I was you, Mrs. Claus."

Her brown eyes warmed with laughter.

He had never wanted to kiss a woman the way he wanted to kiss her. And he'd definitely never used as much self-control as he did at that moment.

"Mrs. Claus, if I wasn't a gentleman..."

Her brows raised a notch and she backed up. "I think we should go find the children."

He closed his eyes, one last attempt at chivalry. He brushed past her, grazing next to her ear with a kiss she wouldn't feel.

"Ho, ho, ho! Merry Christmas!" He shouted as he walked away and left her standing in the tiny hall outside the bathroom. Kids shouted and somewhere a dog barked.

Man, he was falling hard and fast.

As he walked down the hall to the activity room, Elizabeth behind him, he managed to get it together. He put a jolly smile on his face and braced himself for twenty kids tackling him as he walked through the door.

Behind him, Mrs. Claus let out a screech as the tackle advanced and kids circled her, hugging her tight. He smiled and watched as she settled into her role, hugging the kids back, listening as they told her all about Christmas. One of the kids tugged at her arm and said something about Christmas really being about Jesus.

He thought his Santa suit would burst with pride. Until yesterday she'd been nothing but a name, a story. The fact that she was hugging these kids, his kids, shouldn't matter. But it did. For some crazy reason, it did.

Jemma pointed him toward the chair she'd set up for him. He sat down, arranging the pillow he'd shoved under the jacket of his costume.

A little girl holding Elizabeth's hand led her to the nativity the kids had put up on a table next to the Christmas tree. As the child pointed and talked, Elizabeth leaned to listen.

If ever a woman had needed a little Christmas cheer, it had to be Elizabeth Harden. More than that, he thought, she needed faith. But how did he help her find faith at Christmas?

Chapter Four

Drained. Elizabeth didn't know why that word described her emotions as she left Samaritan House. She glanced back before driving away. Her heart squeezed a little. The kids in that home shouldn't be smiling, laughing, full of joy. They were sucked into a system of foster care and group homes. Most would never return to their biological parents. And yet, they smiled. Oh, did they smile.

She brushed at tears, ashamed but somehow uplifted. She had so much and she took it for granted. These children had found happiness and were loved at Christmas.

She'd skipped Christmas at times, letting go of tradition. Maybe because her family didn't have small children in their lives to remind them to keep the traditions, to keep the meaning of the holiday. Way back in her memory she snagged hold of a childhood memory of loving Christmas. The lights, the trees, even an occasional church service on Christmas Eve.

"You okay?" Travis leaned against the passenger door of the truck, allowing him to stretch his leg.

"I'm good." She sniffled a little. "Thank you for letting me be Mrs. Claus today."

"Yeah, I knew you'd love it once you got there."

"I did." She turned back toward the bed-and-breakfast. "What happens now? I mean, do you buy them gifts or does someone else? What about the event last night? Does the money have to be refunded to the ticket holders?"

She had a list of questions ticking through her mind. He raised a hand, stopping her.

"It'll get done."

That answer caused her to get a little itchy. It sounded like a plan without having a plan. "But how?"

"Are you worried?" He pointed for her to turn right. "You love being organized, don't you?"

"It does make me feel better if I have a plan and I know what needs to happen."

"Right, I work better off the cuff. But don't worry, it'll get done."

"Christmas is two weeks away."

"Yes, it is." He glanced at his watch. "That's scary."

She had to let it go. Her responsibility had been to travel to Tulsa and represent Harden Industries, nothing more. Represent, make an appearance. Now it was time to go home, not worry about when or how the gifts would be bought.

But she couldn't stop thinking about those children and the lists they'd given Travis. They wanted the normal toys: trucks, dolls and games. They had also asked for a new stove for Jemma and a truck for Dutch. They'd asked for gifts for siblings not placed with them, and for parents they rarely got to see.

"I need to call the airport and see if I can get a flight this evening."

"Yeah, I kind of forgot about that. I need to see if Uri can drive me back to Dawson." He stared at her for a long minute. "Or you could drive me. And then you'd be around to make sure I got everything done. We wouldn't want the kids to go without gifts."

He was baiting her. She knew it. And yet…what if he didn't get everything done? It wasn't her problem. But she kept remembering that little girl who had hugged her tight. Becka had just turned five. Her parents had lost their parental rights permanently.

The Coopers had invited her to stay with them, at their home in Dawson. Why not? What did she really have in St. Louis? She could go to the office. She could write thank-you cards for wedding gifts she would return. And then what?

"The house is at the end of this block." Travis broke into her wandering thoughts. "Relax, I was teasing. I really do have a plan for getting everything done."

"I know."

Elizabeth pulled the truck up the long drive to his

aunt's bed-and-breakfast. The big Victorian home was cream-colored with sage-green trim. Wicker furniture lined the porch that wrapped around the front and one side of the house.

"I'll drive you home." She parked the truck and avoided looking at him. "I can get a ride back to Tulsa, right? And maybe fly out tomorrow or the next day?"

"Of course." He cleared his throat. "You could go over my list, check it twice and make sure I'm organized enough."

"I'm sure you're organized. The thing you can't do is drive yourself."

"Right, concussion and sprained ankle." He opened his door and grabbed the crutches as he got out. "You'll love Dawson. You might even want to spend Christmas with us. After all, the kids will be expecting Mrs. Claus when Santa returns with their gifts."

"Yeah, I think you'll have to explain that Mrs. Claus had to go back to the North Pole."

"Okay, but you'll break their hearts." He waited for her to join him and they walked up to the house together.

She didn't want to think about broken hearts, neither hers nor the hearts of the children she'd met that day. If she stayed here, drove him home, helped with the gifts, that would keep her busy and keep her from thinking about Richard. Would it be so bad, staying away from St. Louis for a few extra days?

Then she'd go home. She'd have to face her life eventually.

At the door Travis shifted the crutches, leaning them against the wall. Elizabeth looked up, questioning what he was up to now. His expression shifted, softening the laughter that normally sparkled in those eyes of his.

"Are you okay? You know I'm teasing, right? I do that, sometimes too much." His words were soft, with an easy, sweet smile.

She couldn't get the words out. She'd never felt so out of control. She'd never been emotional. And now, tears streamed down her cheeks and her throat tightened painfully. She blinked to clear her vision. Before she could brush the tears away, Travis touched her cheek. Tenderly, with hands that were gentle but rough, he cupped her cheeks. His gaze captured hers, holding her frozen to the spot.

She closed her eyes, unsure of how it could be this way, with a stranger comforting her.

"It will get easier. It'll hurt less."

His words were raspy and uneven. Did he know for sure that it would get easier? Did he know that she didn't want to go back to St. Louis because she didn't want the sympathetic looks people had been giving her for the last week? How did Elizabeth Harden get left for someone her fiancé picked up at the perfume counter?

Elizabeth thought the girl Richard left her for was beautiful. She looked like a person anyone would want to know. Her name was Tonya and she looked fun and happy. Tonya looked like someone who didn't have lists and schedules. Tonya probably had time for picnics and Saturday afternoon drives.

"I'm sorry," she whispered, sniffling as she tried to stop the surge of emotion. It didn't work.

The tears continued to stream down her cheeks. Travis wrapped his arms around her and pulled her close. Elizabeth let him pull her against a strong chest, hold her in strong arms. His flannel shirt was soft beneath her cheek, soaking up her tears. His hands rubbed her back and he whispered into her hair that she would make it through this.

No one had ever held her the way he was holding her, as if she was the most fragile, precious thing in the world. She'd always been too strong for that kind of tenderness.

After a few minutes he brushed a kiss across the top of her head and he let go, unwrapping his arms, stepping back. Elizabeth wiped the last tears from her cheeks.

"I can't believe I did that. I'm so sorry." She closed her eyes and avoided looking at him. "I don't fall apart like that, it's just…"

"You're really going to make excuses? Why?"

"Because I'm fine. I don't have a broken heart. I'm not going to fall apart."

It made her mad that he looked sorry. For her. "I think it's okay to fall apart once in a while."

"Oh, do you fall apart often?"

He brushed his hand through her hair, tangling his fingers in flyaway strands. Finally he smiled, his eyes crinkling at the corners. "Never."

"Of course not." She opened the door. "I'll still drive you home."

"Thank you. And if I ever fall apart, you're the first person I'll turn to."

She looked back at him and she allowed herself to be pulled into a lighter mood generated by his humor. "If you ever need to be held, I'll be here."

"In that case, I'm going to fall apart soon. And often."

He made it easy to smile. The cowboy who had flirted, rescued her from a bull and held children as if they were the most precious things in the world had somehow, in just a matter of days, become a friend.

She explained to herself that this wouldn't last. She'd drive him home and then she'd return to her home, her life. A simple plan that she meant to stick to because all of this was temporary, even the quick beat of her heart when his hand touched her back— temporary.

Slick roads had kept them another night at Uri and Yelena's. A night with the two of them stuck together in Yelena's rose-scented parlor, listening to Uri snore as Yelena knitted a scarf. They'd glance at one another occasionally, hiding smiles when Yelena would look up from her yarn. It had been a long night.

Now they were home. Travis couldn't help but relax a little as the truck pulled up the driveway and his parents' home came into view. It always felt good to get back here to his life and routine.

Horses grazed in the fields, nibbling at grass now brown from winter weather. Winter did that to Oklahoma—painted it shades of brown and gray. The trees, the sky, the grass. But touches of blue and green put color back in the landscape. The green of a cedar tree. The blue of the sky when the winter storm ended.

The colors itched inside him, waiting to be painted. He had studied the woman behind the wheel of his truck. He thought about her in the midst of a gray-and-brown canvas, her auburn hair, the deep red of her sweater. Yeah, he'd paint her. He'd capture her with that smile, the one that said she had forgotten for a minute that she'd been hurt.

The way she'd smiled when the children at Samaritan House surrounded her with hugs and laughter.

The way she smiled when he whispered that she should always be Mrs. Claus. He'd been teasing because that's what he did. But the teasing had changed, without his even knowing how or why, the teasing had become too much like what he wanted.

He had a sudden empathy for fish, because when they were snagged and being reeled in, they must feel a little like he felt. He was getting pulled toward something and he didn't know what.

"It's beautiful." Elizabeth's observation brought everything back to focus.

The house ahead of them, two-story brick, white columns across the front porch. He remembered back more than twenty years, the first time he'd seen it. He had thought it had to be another orphanage. It had scared him silly at five, this big house and all of the Coopers who had waited on the front porch.

"Yeah, it's pretty amazing." He unbuckled his seat belt as she pulled around the circle drive and parked.

The front door opened. His mom stood in the entry, waving, her smile huge and welcoming. She'd been thrilled when he called and told her that Elizabeth would drive him home. She'd been a little too thrilled. Yeah, the matchmaker in her had to be working overtime. She'd always told them that she had a dozen kids because she wanted several dozen grandchildren.

No pressure.

She hadn't been thrilled to hear of him falling and the concussion that had caused him to lose his balance. She should be used to it. It wasn't as if injuries weren't a pretty common thing for the Cooper guys.

He walked with Elizabeth, maneuvering ice and patches of snow. Elizabeth had insisted on stopping at a department store and picking up a few things. Not that he blamed her. She'd brought one change of clothes to Tulsa and he knew, from experience with his sisters, that a woman needed way more than that. She carried her purchases in a new, bright red suitcase.

"Welcome to Cooper Creek, Elizabeth." His mom hugged their guest and led her into the house. Travis smiled. That's what his mom did, she brought everyone into their house.

Which might explain why he'd turned the bunkhouse into an apartment. He had his space, a place that went undisturbed and where he could escape the crowds. He hadn't lived in the main house for over ten years, not since his seventeenth birthday. That's when his dad had helped him finish the renovations on the forgotten apartment attached to the stable.

"Thank you, Mrs. Cooper." Elizabeth followed his mother to the kitchen. "I appreciate your taking me in for a day or two."

"Oh, honey, we want you for more than a day or two. There's no reason for you to rush off when Christmas is just around the corner and your parents are—" his mom patted Elizabeth's arm "—well, out of the country."

"I do have to get back to St. Louis. With my dad gone, I'm sure there will be situations I need to take care of for him."

"Well, we'd love for you to stay as long as you like." His mom poured two cups of coffee. "Are you tired? I'm sure you've had a long couple of days, driving Trav around, playing Mrs. Claus and then the trip to Dawson."

"I'm not at all tired." Elizabeth turned to look at him. "You don't have to stay with me."

"I have to leave," he looked at his watch, "in thirty minutes."

"Don't you think you should put your foot up?"

"No, I'm fine. I have to ditch these crutches, though." He finished his coffee.

"Who's going to drive you over to Back Street?" His mom looked a little worried. "I don't know if your dad or Jackson is at the barn, but one of them could take you over."

"I can drive myself."

Elizabeth cleared her throat. "Where is it you have to go?"

"Dawson Community Center is putting on a live nativity for Christmas. I'm helping with props and scenery. It has to be finished this week."

"Oh, well, I don't mind helping."

"Are you sure?" Yeah, a part of him wanted her to go with him. The other part wanted time alone.

"I'm sure, unless you'd rather I didn't." The narrow-eyed look she gave him made him wonder if she could read his thoughts.

"No, that would be great. I'm going to go down to my place and get ready. We'll leave in about thirty minutes."

His mom clapped her hands together and smiled. "That's perfect. That'll give me time to show Elizabeth to her room."

Yeah, perfect. Travis couldn't think of anything

less perfect than his mom alone with Elizabeth, talking about him and plotting. He smiled, though. Let her have her fun. Elizabeth didn't plan on staying long, so it wasn't as if his mom would get anywhere.

As he walked out the front door, he heard his mom say his favorite words—"and this is a picture of Trav." He was six years old, and his brothers dressed him up like a hula dancer.

Chapter Five

After getting settled, Elizabeth got directions from Angie Cooper and headed for the stable to find Travis. She walked down the driveway, steering clear of the spots still covered with ice and snow. The sun sank on the western horizon, painting the sky shades of lavender and pink. She pulled gloves out of her jacket pocket and slipped them on.

As she walked, horses wandered to the fence and then walked along it, following her. In the distance she could see tall fences and bulls grazing on brown winter grass. A truck eased through the back of the field and cattle walked behind it. Elizabeth stopped to watch and after a few minutes she hurried on to the barn.

Stable or barn? It was a huge metal building and as she stepped inside she saw that it held a high-ceilinged arena and on one side, stalls for horses. Music drifted down from the far end of the building.

That had to be the bunkhouse apartment where Travis lived.

The music got louder. She hesitated outside the door listening to old rock but finally rapped lightly. A few minutes later he opened it, looking pretty disheveled. Earlier he'd been wearing contacts. He'd replaced them with the dark-framed glasses he sometimes wore. His smile didn't really welcome her. In fact, she got the feeling she might have overstepped her boundaries.

"I'm sorry, I didn't know if you were coming back up to the house." She was not a teenager with a crush, so why did she stumble over her words and sound as if she'd just bumped into the cutest guy in school without meaning to?

He stepped back and motioned her inside. "Come in. I lost track of time."

Elizabeth stepped into Travis Cooper's world. A cluttered, kind-of-crazy world. The living area and kitchen were one huge room and had the look of a loft apartment she'd once rented. But this apartment was attached to a barn. She smiled as she looked around, going from the black leather furniture, modern, not country, to the white cabinets and black counters of the kitchen. And then chaos. Next to the kitchen the loft look ended and mayhem reigned.

There were easels, canvases leaning against paint-splattered walls and bright lights.

"What in the world?" She turned to face her host.

"My art studio."

"You paint?"

He laughed and took her by the hand. "I paint. It's

always kept me out of trouble. When life gets crazy, when my brain won't settle down, or as a kid when I couldn't stay out of trouble, painting gets me back on track."

"When your brain won't settle down?" She studied a painting, of a bull in the arena, foam and dirt, a cowboy gripping the rope. It was abstract with wide splashes of browns and reds, like a camera unable to focus on a fast-moving subject. "This is really good."

"For a country boy?"

"I didn't mean it that way. I just wouldn't have thought of you as an artist."

"I don't know that I'm an artist. It's more that I have to keep busy and this is how my energy is best channeled."

"You seem settled to me."

He picked up a box and filled it with paints, brushes and pencils. "That would be the medicine."

"Medicine?"

"I'm ADHD, have been my whole life." He led her past a canvas with a setting similar to the one outside. Gold and brown grass, a winter sky and a bare spot in the center. "Sit. I thought I'd outgrow the ADHD. You know, like it was just something that happened to kids who were hyper. But I've learned that it's who I am and it isn't going away."

She sat on the stool that he pulled into place and pointed to. He left her and stepped back behind the canvas. Shouldn't she be expecting the unexpected by now?

"Shouldn't we be going?"

"Later."

"I thought…"

He raised a hand, paintbrush in his mouth while he studied the canvas. She started to ask him why she needed to sit and he raised a hand to stop her again.

"Give me thirty minutes and we'll go. I'll even buy you dinner at the Mad Cow."

"Mad Cow." She leaned, wishing she could see what he was doing to a landscape that obviously depicted the countryside around them. Why would he need for her to sit? Well, that was obvious, but she didn't want to be in the center of his landscape.

"Hold still." He glanced around the edge of the canvas. "Maybe look off over your right shoulder, like you just spotted something interesting."

"I'm a business major, not a model."

"Right, I get that. Now smile a little, if you don't mind."

"What's the Mad Cow?" She shifted as he'd asked and looked to the side.

"The only restaurant in town, unless you want an egg roll or corn dog from the convenience store."

"Yummy."

"Hey, don't knock it." He winked and went back to work. "He missed out, you know."

He? Oh, Richard. She didn't want to talk about losing her fiancé days before her wedding. Why did Travis want to bring it up? She sighed and turned to face him, to study his face, his serious expression.

"I don't think he missed out," she admitted, a little to herself, a little to Travis. "I mean, he obviously didn't love me. And he really seems to love her. That isn't missing out, is it?"

"I think it is." He dabbed the brush into paint and went back to work. "I think he missed out."

Her heart did a crazy, unexpected twirl. Reality would get it back on track, make it less likely to make something out of nothing. Travis Cooper was a player, very much like the one who had left her. They knew how to say sweet things when it mattered, and break a girl's heart as if it didn't.

"Should we go shopping for gifts tomorrow, for the children at Samaritan House?"

Travis shook his head. "Stop worrying. This isn't my first year doing this."

"But there are so many of them and Christmas is just around the corner."

"I know that. Put away your pocket organizer and relax."

"That's mean." She scooted off the stool. "We should go. It's almost six o'clock."

Travis glanced at his watch and mumbled something she couldn't hear and he kept painting. "I'm almost finished."

"Should I be afraid?"

He grinned and shook his head. She studied him, the cute and studious-looking cowboy. At the bull riding event she'd put him in the category of "cowboys who like to have a good time." Now she had to rethink her stereotype.

He dressed like Santa for children in a group home and he painted. He knew how to hug a woman in a way that made her want to stay in his arms because his arms were a safe place.

Yeah, she should be afraid.

"You can look now." Travis stepped back from the canvas, pleased because he'd managed to capture what he'd envisioned just a short time earlier. He had captured the lost look in her eyes.

Elizabeth stepped next to him, all serious and worried, her brows scrunched together. He smiled down at her as she studied the painting.

"I look sad."

He studied the portrait of a woman standing in a field, just the way he'd imagined her. The dark red of her sweater, auburn hair blowing in a light breeze, straw-colored grass dotted with snow.

"No, not sad. You're looking for something." He turned to drop his brush in cleaner.

"Really? What do you think I'm looking for?"

He picked up a rag and wiped his hands. "That's something you have to figure out."

"Oh, aren't you mysterious."

"I've heard a little mystery gets a woman's attention."

Elizabeth picked up her purse and headed for the

door. "This woman deals in cold, hard facts and punctuality. We should go."

"Elizabeth, it was a joke."

"I'm not here looking for something, Travis. I'm here because my flight got canceled." She sighed. "And because my parents are on my honeymoon. And because my fiancé eloped with a woman he met while buying a gift. For me. I'm not looking for anything. I'm really just looking for a way to get home and back to my life."

"I can help you do that, tomorrow."

Her expression softened. "I'm sorry. I didn't mean to lose it. You've been nothing but kind."

Travis thought about that and he laughed. "I'm pretty sure I haven't been kind. For the most part I've been thinking that some bozo made a huge mistake, and that I'm really glad he did."

"Oh. Well. We should really go."

Travis agreed. They should go. And he should learn to keep his mouth shut. All his life people had called him charming. At the moment, he strongly disagreed. In the opinion of the woman next to him, he was anything but charming.

They were driving toward Back Street when she smiled at him. Yeah, her fiancé had been an idiot. Travis couldn't imagine walking away from this woman with her lacy, crocheted stocking cap pulled down on auburn hair and those big eyes all soft and sweet.

"It's a beautiful painting."

"I had a beautiful subject." He took one hand off the wheel and slapped his forehead. "I'm sorry, I said I wouldn't do that anymore."

"You're a flirt. I think you can't help it."

He slid a glance her way. "For most of my life, yeah."

"You've never had a serious relationship? A woman who made you want to settle down?"

He could tell her that he hadn't, but today things were different. He could honestly say that he'd never felt that way after a few days with a woman. Not that he hadn't wanted to feel that way. It just hadn't happened before.

"Yes, I've met a woman who did that to me. It isn't someone I know very well." He turned into the parking lot of Dawson Community Center, formerly Back Street Church. "But I'm not good at relationships."

"Maybe you haven't met the right person."

Travis eased into a parking space and cut the engine of his truck. "Yeah, maybe I haven't. I've always been told when the right woman comes along, I'll know."

"Yes, just make sure you know before you propose to the wrong woman."

"I'll try to remember that." He opened his door and looked out at the church lawn that had somehow turned into the ancient city of Bethlehem.

Elizabeth studied it as well. "This is amazing. The people in town did this?"

"Yeah, the kids who hang out here and the local churches all worked together on it. I have a few details to add on the inn and then we'll head over to the Mad Cow."

"I'm still not sure about eating at a restaurant with that name."

He laughed and she got out of the truck. Together they walked up to the church. "Don't worry, there's nowhere better than the Mad Cow for good, home-style cooking."

"So, I shouldn't be afraid."

He reached for her hand. "No, my little city friend, you shouldn't be afraid."

Her fingers clasped his. "Of course not."

But her fingers were tight and he thought she trembled.

"This is the Dawson Community Center." He figured it might be a good time to change the subject. "Formerly Back Street Church, it sat empty for years until Jeremy Hightree bought it."

They walked through the front door of the church. It was ablaze with lights and echoed with activity. One of the local teens shouted and a few waved. They were decorating for the beginning of the nativity.

"What is it they're going to do here?"

"Starting a week before Christmas they'll have nightly tours of Bethlehem, and a living nativity."

"A play?"

"Well, yes, I guess. A play based on the birth of Jesus."

She grew silent and he had a lot of his own questions for her. Her loneliness went way beyond a broken engagement. Only days ago he'd still been the guy who didn't mind empty conversation. He'd been the guy who really didn't want to get involved.

Today, he wanted to find a way to never let a woman down. And that was pretty much a problem for a guy like him.

"Hey, Travis, there you are." A woman had come up the stairs. She was small with dark hair that fell past her shoulders. Her smile included Elizabeth. "And you brought help!"

"Help for what?" Travis still had hold of her hand. "Can't you keep my brother in line?"

"It isn't Jeremy, it's the kids down here making cookies. We're taking cookies to shut-ins and to the nursing home. Tomorrow."

"Tomorrow?" Travis let go of Elizabeth's hand to lean and hug the other woman. "You're crazy, taking all this on."

"Someone has to do it." She smiled at Elizabeth and held out a hand. "I'm Beth Hightree."

"Elizabeth Harden."

"Welcome to Dawson. I hope you're up for some craziness. We're in the process of making cookies and doing last-minute alterations on costumes."

"Count me out on cookies, I have to finish painting the inn." Travis gave Elizabeth a little push. "But I bet Elizabeth is a Christmas cookie expert."

"Uh, no, she isn't." Elizabeth shot him a look that he seemed intent on ignoring. "Really, I can tell you where to buy some lovely cookies, but making them is a skill I don't have."

"You'll be great." He started backing away.

Elizabeth grabbed his hand. "But you're going to stay and help."

"I have an inn to build."

"Don't leave me alone," she whispered even though everyone could hear.

His gray eyes twinkled and he grinned. "You can't live without me? Is that what you're saying?"

"No, it isn't at all what I'm saying." She didn't have a person, someone to count on, to hold on to. At the moment, he was her person. He had to know that.

For years she'd been so caught up in her schooling and her career that she'd lost track of true friends. She'd had business associates, coworkers and then Richard.

Until Richard walked out on their engagement she hadn't realized how solitary she'd become. Not until she tried calling people she considered friends and no one came. No one spent an evening with her, took her to lunch or spent a night watching chick flicks with her to cheer her up.

She watched movies alone, eating ice cream from

the container and wishing she had friends like the ones in the movies.

What a sad reflection on her life that this man, a stranger, had become her person.

As she stood there, trying to be her strong self, unemotional and capable, his expression changed. His gaze connected with hers. He nodded a little and his smile didn't mock, it said he got it.

Elizabeth breathed deep and let go of his hand. She turned and Beth Hightree had a funny smile on her face.

"We'll both help you with cookies." Travis opened a door that led downstairs to a basement. "I'll come back tomorrow and work on the inn."

Beth went ahead of them, leaving them for just a minute together at the top of the steps. Travis glanced down at her, his teasing smile completely gone.

"You okay?"

"I'm good. I just…" She wasn't going to say she needed him. "I don't know anyone."

"You don't seem like the shy type."

"I might be. I've never been given the opportunity."

He smiled again, disarming, off-putting, charming. There were so many words to describe that cowboy's smile.

"So, shy is a new skill you're trying out? If you get the opportunity?"

"I'm used to my world. I know where I belong there and where I fit."

"Do you?"

Did he have to do that? Two little words and she no longer knew about herself. She really had an urge to slug him in the gut.

"You're horrible." That was the best she could do.

He tilted his straw cowboy hat that seemed at odds with the dark-framed glasses. The studious cowboy. Did he know who he was?

"You're my person," she whispered as he took hold of her hand and led her down the stairs.

"I'm your what?"

"Nothing. But thank you for not leaving me on my own."

"You got it, city girl. I won't leave you alone."

She wondered if he knew that she was going to hold him to that.

Not that it mattered over the next hour if he stayed by her side or not. Beth Hightree kept them so busy that Elizabeth didn't have a chance to think about being alone, or what she'd do with herself when she went back to St. Louis.

They decorated cookies. Bells, angels, Christmas trees, snowmen and stars. Frosting, colored sugar and sprinkles were everywhere.

"This is fun." She spread a dab of white frosting on a star and sprinkled it with yellow sugar.

Travis had left for a minute, just to do inventory on the work left to do on the inn. Beth had taken his place next to her.

"It's fun for an hour or so. After two or three—"

Beth straightened and lifted her arms "—it's a pain in the back."

Elizabeth liked Beth and her husband, Jeremy, the long-lost Cooper brother. Travis had told her the story, the condensed version, he said. Yeah, if she lived in Dawson, Beth could be a friend. She would be the kind of person a girl counted on, watched movies with or ate an entire container of ice cream with.

"Okay, I have a confession." Elizabeth placed her decorated star on the platter with the finished cookies.

"Does this have something to do with Travis?" Beth's eyes widened.

Heat rushed its way up Elizabeth's cheeks. "No! Actually, I was only going to tell you that I've never made Christmas cookies."

Beth's cheeks turned a little pink. "Oh, well, that's not at all like the secret I imagined."

"No, I guess it isn't."

"But you've seriously never made Christmas cookies? How could you not?"

"I guess it wasn't something we did. I have other secrets that are just as disturbing. Like I haven't put a tree up in three years."

"That is pretty disturbing."

"I could think of more, but I think that's enough for one day."

Beth bit down on her bottom lip and her eyes narrowed. She went back to work on a pretty bell cookie.

Elizabeth didn't know what to say. It was Beth who broke the silence as she put her finished cookie on the platter.

"I don't know how to ask, but don't you celebrate Christmas?"

Elizabeth shrugged. "I guess it depends on how you view celebrating Christmas. Yes, we celebrate, just quietly. We traveled a lot for the holidays. For years it's been the time of the year that we get away somewhere warm."

"I see." Beth reached for a decorated cookie and handed one to Elizabeth. "I think we should eat one."

"Should we?"

"Definitely. It's the frosting that makes them so wonderful. And the sprinkles." Beth took a bite of the cookie and Elizabeth did the same.

And she had to admit, the cookies were wonderful. They were sweet and sugary with vanilla frosting.

Beth finished hers first. "We had a few very quiet Christmases after my mom died. Dad wouldn't let us go to church. It was hard, not having that connection."

"I'm sorry."

"It was a long time ago." Beth handed her another cookie and Elizabeth shook her head.

"We rarely go to church." She shrugged at the confession and looked around. "Christmas is a holiday, but nothing like this."

"Yeah, it's pretty special to us."

"I can see that."

"Elizabeth, if you need someone to talk to," Beth offered with a sweet smile. "I'm here."

"Thank you. I appreciate that. But really, I'm okay."

"Beth, are you getting all sentimental with my new bestie?"

Elizabeth turned and gave Travis what she hoped would be a withering smile. He didn't wither. Instead he winked and slipped an arm around her waist, pulling her to his side.

"Ready to go, city girl?"

"I have a name." She didn't mind, though. And she didn't mind being held close to his side.

But Travis played the field, she reminded herself. He knew how to make a woman melt. He knew how to tease. He knew how to charm.

She reminded herself that he also knew how to be there for her. Even though he didn't have to be.

"Did you finish what you needed to do?" She slipped from his embrace and turned to Beth. "Are there more cookies?"

"We're done." Beth shot Travis a serious warning look. He didn't seem to notice. If he did, he didn't show it.

"Then let's see if we can't scrounge up some leftovers back at the house." He glanced at his watch. "No way is the Mad Cow still open."

"Take sandwiches from the fridge, Trav." Beth pointed to the big avocado dinosaur of a refrigerator. "We bought deli sandwiches for earlier. There's plenty left."

Travis helped himself, taking a couple of wrapped sandwiches from the fridge. "Later, Beth."

When they walked out the front door of the church, the temperature had dropped drastically. The sky was black as ink, not a star in sight. Elizabeth shivered in her light coat and Travis reached to pull her next to him, to his warmth.

"You should have bought a heavier coat."

Somehow they were no longer moving. They stood facing one another next to his truck. The cold darkness surrounded them. And silence—heavy, heavy silence.

St. Louis was never this dark, this silent.

The air in St. Louis never felt this heavy, this charged with electricity.

Travis held her in his arms, wrapping his coat around her and pulling her into his embrace. His mouth stopped just inches from hers.

"Would you be totally offended if I kissed you?" he whispered, his voice softly accented and husky, with just a slight catch of emotion.

She breathed deep and his scent swept around her, clean, brisk, holding her close. "I think I'd be hurt if you didn't."

"Man, I don't know if I've ever…" He didn't say more. Instead he leaned in, his cold lips touching hers and then warming as the kiss lingered.

He brushed his lips across her cheek, nuzzled her ear, held her close. And then he kissed her again. Eyes closed, she drifted in the dark night, holding on to a moment that wouldn't last forever. Moments like this rarely did.

Their lips separated. He leaned close, whispering near her ear, "You taste like sugar cookies. Do you always taste like cookies?"

"Hmm, no, I don't think so."

"I might have to kiss you again, just to see for sure. Maybe tomorrow."

"I'm going home tomorrow." She'd never been more sad to say those words.

"We'll see about that. I really think you should stay. No onc should be alone at Christmas."

She couldn't agree more. But her heart had already been broken once and she didn't think it could take being hurt by him. Because if he broke it, she thought it might be broken for good.

And she'd finally accepted that what she'd felt after Richard's phone call hadn't been a broken heart. It had been about relief. Anger and betrayal, but also relief.

She'd been spared marriage to a man she hadn't loved, not with her whole heart.

Chapter Six

Bright sunlight streamed through the window of the upstairs bedroom Angie Cooper had shown Elizabeth to the previous day, when she'd first arrived in Dawson. Had it really just been a day? She lay there in the big sleigh bed, trying to make sense of everything that happened the previous evening.

The kiss. Even after they'd shared sandwiches in the big kitchen, alone because Angie and Tim Cooper had already gone to bed, Elizabeth had still remembered the way Travis held her. The way his kiss made her want to believe that someone could really love her forever.

She'd watched him walk out to his truck and drive to his apartment. She'd watched as the lights went out. She'd finally climbed the stairs to the guest room and she'd spent another hour sitting next to the window wondering if God really was out there somewhere, caring about her.

And she'd wondered what Travis had planned to say but hadn't. He'd never what?

Not that it mattered. With morning came new perspective. She'd be leaving. Travis would forget her. Life would go back to normal. Soon. What she needed to do was immerse herself in work and let that be her focus.

As she lay there, a dog barked, doors slammed and then loud voices combined in an uproar that sounded as much like a fight as a party. Someone knocked on her door.

"I'm up." She pulled her blanket to her chin, in case the person on the other side decided to open the door.

"I wanted to let you know that we're making pancakes and then we're going to find our Christmas tree. Do you want to join us?" Angie Cooper's voice on the other side of the door sounded bright and rested.

Elizabeth felt as if she hadn't slept two hours. Her eyes were heavy with sleep and her stomach growled. She'd never been a morning person. But pancakes?

"I'll be down in a few minutes."

"Good. I found warm clothes for you. Can I bring them in?"

"Of course."

The door opened a crack and Angie peeked in. She smiled, looking much younger than a woman with a dozen children, a few of whom were in their thirties. "I think these should fit. And Travis said you needed a warmer coat. I found one of Heather's."

"Thank you."

Angie set the pile of clothes on a nearby chair. "I left the shoes downstairs."

"That's good. I appreciate this so much."

Angie stood next to the bed. "It's the least we can do. I hope you'll enjoy yourself. And really, Elizabeth, you don't have to rush off if you don't want to.

"I appreciate that, but I'd hate to impose."

Angie laughed at her objection. "Honey, you haven't met everyone. You'll see that one extra isn't an imposition. Which reminds me, I need to call my son Jackson because he has one or two more of his own to add to our holidays."

"Oh, is he married?"

"No, and he says he isn't getting married. But life has a way of changing our plans." Angie walked to the door. "It seems my son might be the proud father of a bouncing baby girl—of fourteen."

Angie Cooper said it as if she wasn't shocked. Elizabeth blinked a few times, plenty surprised by the way the other woman made the announcement and then out the door she went.

Mass chaos was the only way to describe the scene in the kitchen when Elizabeth walked in fifteen minutes later. There were kids on the floor playing and a few people sitting at the long table that stretched nearly the width of the room.

Angie Cooper piled pancakes on plates while Travis poured batter on a griddle. He nodded in her direction and went back to work, flipping and then removing pancakes from the griddle.

As if last night had never happened. She called herself a fool for believing it meant something to him. She'd seen him at the bull riding event, flirting with every woman who crossed his path. She'd watched him charm, cajole and tease.

Of course one kiss in the moonlight meant nothing. And it didn't really mean that much to her, either.

"Do you like chocolate chips?" he called out, and she guessed he was talking to her. Everyone else ignored the question.

"Chocolate chips?" She drew closer, watching as he sprinkled chocolate chips onto the pancakes that were already golden brown.

"On your pancakes." He reached back into the bag.

"Oh, I think I might."

"You don't know?"

She shook her head. And watched as he drizzled more chocolate chips on the pancakes.

"You'll have to try them." He flipped pancakes onto the plate his mother had set next to the griddle and then he handed the plate to Elizabeth. "Syrup and butter on the table. There's fresh coffee."

He pointed to a machine that looked as if it belonged in a restaurant. A woman close to Elizabeth's age held a cup under the nozzle and filled it with coffee.

"Do you want some coffee?" She held the cup out to Elizabeth.

"I'd love some, but I can get it. I don't want to take yours."

"I don't drink coffee." The pretty blonde held out the cup. "I'm Heather, kid five in the Cooper clan."

"Hi, Heather, I'm Elizabeth Harden."

"I know the ice storm was kind of disastrous, but I'm glad you can spend Christmas with us."

Elizabeth blinked a few times. She had a cup of coffee in one hand and a plate of pancakes in the other, and really no idea what to say to Heather Cooper. She glanced around, at the crowd of Coopers, at the box with ornaments spilling out, waiting to be hung on the family Christmas tree.

"Oh, I can't stay. I have to get home to..." She didn't even have a cat to use as an excuse.

A low chuckle behind her. She turned, glancing up into Travis's laughing eyes fringed with dark lashes. "What, you have a cat to feed?"

How did he do that? He just shrugged and reached past her for a prescription medicine bottle at the back of the cabinet.

"I don't have a cat, I have..." Nothing. Oh, good grief, that sounded pitiful. She'd always been very happy with her life. Content.

"You have what?" Travis smelled good. He stood close, his arm brushing hers. His hair was a mess and he had flour on his T-shirt and arms.

She stared up at the man, speechless. He pulled off his dark-framed glasses and wiped them with the hem of his T-shirt, lifted them and then wiped them again before placing them back on a nose that had just a hint of a bump. It was good that he wasn't perfect.

"I have things to do." She had set her plate on the counter to pour syrup over the pancakes. She picked it up, took the fork that Heather offered and walked away.

When she sat down at the big dining room table, small Cooper kids on either side of her, Travis remained in her field of vision. He swallowed a pill from the bottle, washed it down with water and went back to making pancakes.

"He's a nuisance." Heather sat down across from her. "You'd like Reese. He's in the army, though. Jackson isn't here yet. Blake is busy with something at the bank."

Was Heather purposely listing all the single Cooper men?

Well, Elizabeth had never been one to hint. "Heather, I'm sure they're all very nice, but I just ended my engagement last week."

Heather patted her arm. "I'm sorry, I didn't mean to pry or push single brothers at you. I should really know better. People are constantly trying to fix me up. I enjoy being single."

"It does have its advantages." Being single meant not being left at the altar. Being single meant not worrying that another person would hurt her.

"It must have been difficult."

"It did take me by surprise."

"I think that's probably an understatement." Heather took a fork from one of the children next to Elizabeth. The little boy was about to stab the table. "Enough of that, guys. Scratch Nana's table and there will be trouble."

Elizabeth took her last bite of pancake and stood to take her plate to the sink. Travis stood at the sink helping his mother do the dishes. "I can help with those."

She'd expected Travis to step away and let her take his place. Instead his mother stepped away.

"If you don't mind," Angie smiled. "I need to make sure Tim has blankets in the wagons."

"Wagons?" Elizabeth took a plate out of the rinse water and stacked it in the drainer. Travis chuckled, the sound low in his chest.

"Yeah, we Coopers do love our traditions. We have Haflingers..."

"Haflingers?"

"Small work horses. We hook them to wagons, everyone piles in and we head to the back field where there is a stand of cedar trees."

"Wouldn't it be easier to pick up a tree at the store? They have lovely fake trees that don't require watering."

"City girl, you take all of the fun out of things. Hang with us and you won't want to go back to your 'buy it at the store' lifestyle."

She wanted to argue, but when he helped her into the wagon a short time later, she thought he might have a point. Together, with a dozen or so Coopers, she sat in the bottom of the wagon, leaning against the side rails and huddled under a quilt.

The horses that pulled the wagons were golden-coated with light manes and tails. As they started off through the field, Travis jumped in the back of the wagon she rode in. He eased himself next to her.

"Having fun?" He leaned against the side of the wagon, his legs stretched in front of him and his arm resting behind her head.

"Much better than driving down to the store to buy a tree."

"I told you so."

"And here I thought you weren't the type of guy who would rub it in."

"I wouldn't always. Only when I feel strongly about the point I'm making."

"Which is?" She smiled up at him.

"That you should spend Christmas with the Coopers. I guess I have to remind you that without you and your pocket organizer to help, I'll probably forget to buy gifts for all the children at Samaritan House. Plus they'll be disappointed not to see Mrs. Claus again."

"That's a sad story."

"I know, very sad." He rested his hand on her shoulder.

"I'll think about staying. For the kids' sake. How's your ankle?"

"Good. I have it taped, but I can wear my boots again."

She nodded and let it go.

The wagon creaked along the trail, jostling and bouncing. She definitely wouldn't recommend crossing the country in such a vehicle. She honestly couldn't imagine being an early settler and uprooting her life to move west, traveling by wagon.

Travis's arm draped around her and his hand rested on her arm. All around them people were talking and laughing and she was definitely in new territory.

Travis started the first verse of a Christmas carol and the rest of the family chimed in, the way he'd known they would. Next to him, Elizabeth sang along, hesitating on the words. Her cheeks were pink. Her eyes were bright.

He wished he had a sprig of mistletoe to hold over her head. Any excuse for a repeat of the previous evening and a kiss that had kept him painting into the early hours. He'd put the finishing touches on her portrait and then he'd gone out to the barn and cleaned stalls because he hadn't been able to push thoughts of her from his mind.

It sounded crazy, like a country song, but she did something to him. He hadn't expected that when he pushed her out of the path of that bull the other day.

She moved and he smiled down at her. He could stay right here, in this spot, forever. He could handle this, the quiet, settled person that she brought out in him.

He didn't have a single desire to rush off and find something else to do. He had one goal, spending time next to her. In the wagon, braving cold weather to go chop down a tree seemed like one of the best ways to spend a day.

"Hey, Trav, you're unusually quiet." Mia, his youngest sister, smirked.

"I'm always quiet."

Heather laughed at that. "Trav, you're never quiet. What's up with you? Jesse, do you think he's sick?"

Jesse, his physician brother, had to comment. "It depends on the other symptoms. But I don't think it's contagious."

"This is why I love my family." Travis shot Jesse a warning look. Jesse didn't seem fazed. The family doctor and the family clown, both of them had been adopted the same year. Travis came from Russia. Jesse from South America had been the quiet kid, the studious one, from the very beginning.

"Yeah, we love you, too." Jesse turned his attention to Elizabeth. "Did Travis tell you that we're twins?"

"Twins?" Elizabeth looked from Travis to Jesse. "Really?"

Jesse Alvarez Cooper laughed, white teeth flashing in his dark face. "Yeah, we were adopted the same year. I was older by a few years and we didn't look anything alike, but we've always been pretty close. It's like that when you're a twin. You almost know what the other person is thinking and you even feel what they're feeling."

"Jesse, enough." Heather's quiet voice cut between the two.

"Thanks, sis." Travis shot Jesse another warning look. Usually the sensitive guy, Jesse had gone too far this time. Didn't he get it, that she didn't know how to handle a family like theirs? She hadn't grown up with a dozen siblings, always teasing and going at each other.

Jesse lost his grin but laughter still lurked in his eyes. "I only meant to say that the other night when Trav got knocked in the head, I had a headache."

Travis would have been mad had it not been for Elizabeth's laughter. The sound kind of went all over him, making him feel about a million things at once. Most of all, it made him think that he did have some kind of untreatable illness.

Fortunately things got quiet as the wagon, driven by Lucky, second oldest of the bunch, climbed a slight hill. Just over that hill they would stop and pick a tree from the dozens that dotted the landscape. Cedar trees weren't always the prettiest evergreen, but they smelled about the best.

The wagon jostled to a stop. The tinkle of bells on the horses' harness broke the silence.

"Time to get out," Travis announced as the rest of the group clambered out of the wagon. Elizabeth stood carefully, wobbling a little.

He reached for her hand and led her to the end of the wagon. Heather hopped down, landing next to Jesse. And next went Mia. Elizabeth sat on the edge of the wagon and Jesse stepped forward, but after a quick look from Travis, he backed away. Travis hopped off the back of the wagon, most of his weight on his left leg, saving his right ankle from the impact. It was better but it wasn't healed.

He reached for Elizabeth's hand and she hopped down, landing next to him.

"Your family does this every year?"

"Every year that I can remember. We like our traditions." He led her toward the crowd. And it was a big crowd. Even if they didn't all show up, it still took two wagons. It took a lot to keep a big family close, especially as they got older and moved away.

So they kept the traditions that had been started when the kids were young. They showed up for breakfast each year. They took the wagon to the back field to get a tree. When they got back to the house they'd have the roast his mom put in the Crock-Pot long before dawn, and then they'd decorate the tree.

"It's beautiful out here." Elizabeth turned away from him. "It's snowing."

She smiled big, looking up at the gray sky as big flakes started to fall. The white fluff landed on her stocking cap and melted. It dusted her shoulders and clung to her hair for mere seconds.

"It won't last long. Big flakes like that never last."

"It doesn't matter. It's the moment that counts." She looked up at him, her eyes glittering with dampness, her lips shining with gloss.

Yeah, moments counted. And sometimes moments had to be walked away from him. He needed to walk away.

"Let's find a tree."

"Does everyone agree on one tree?"

Her hand slipped into his.

So much for walking away from the moment.

"We pick one for the main house. But Lucky and his wife pick one for their family. Jesse might get one for his apartment. Mia, too. Heather has a fake silver thing she puts up at her house. Jackson... Who knows about Jackson."

"Gotcha."

The family had headed off into the thickest stand of trees. Travis led Elizabeth toward the group, fighting the urge to lead her off by herself. Yeah, that would not be the smartest thing he'd ever done. It was right up there with the thought that he wished he'd grabbed that sprig of mistletoe.

"You two coming with us?" Jesse glanced back, indicating with a nod that they should catch up.

Travis didn't answer. He had never minded being the kid brother, the clown of the family, Jesse's sidekick. He'd never minded being the guy who rodeoed for a living but had a degree in business.

He had his place in the family; they all did. He got pegged as one of the babies, along with Brian and Mia. Maybe that had been fine at fifteen when he pushed his chores off on the older brothers. At twenty-eight it didn't fit. A family like theirs meant two things: sometimes a kid struggled to be noticed, sometimes they struggled to be alone.

At that moment he wished he and Elizabeth could be anywhere but surrounded by his family.

Chapter Seven

Snow still fell from the light gray sky as the wagon creaked and dipped along the trail that led back to the Cooper house. Elizabeth lifted the twig of cedar she'd pulled from one tree and inhaled the fragrant scent that clung to her gloves and stayed with her, taking a place in her memory that would forever be the smell of Christmas in Oklahoma.

And the man next to her, he would forever be a part of the memory, too. Because he made her think that she could get past what had happened to her.

The wagon stopped in front of the big, two-story brick home.

"All ashore that's going ashore," Lucky shouted from his seat at the front of the wagon. "Guys, help get the tree from the other wagon."

"Ladies, let's get lunch on the table so we can decorate the tree." Heather called out as she climbed down.

This time Elizabeth managed to hop down on her own, landing lightly next to Mia and Heather. They pulled her along with them, including her in their sisterly camaraderie, making her a part of their family, if just for a little while.

Angie Cooper met them at the door. "Come on, girls, let's get the hot chocolate heated up and the table set for lunch."

A few minutes later Elizabeth didn't know where she fit. The Cooper women knew what to do, where to go. As Elizabeth stood in the center of the kitchen, the other women were pulling out plates, silverware, glasses and napkins. They were heating hot chocolate and finding peppermint sticks.

Heather turned from setting the table. "I'm so sorry. We all get so busy doing what we do and we forget that not everyone knows our routine. We need to fill glasses with ice. The glasses are on the counter."

"I can do that." Anything to be useful, to not stand and worry that she might be imposing.

She filled the glasses and carried them on a tray that Angie provided. The table had been set and she put a glass next to each setting. As she finished, a loud bang was heard coming from the front of the house and then loud talking, signaling the arrival of the men with the tree.

"There they are." Heather motioned for her to follow. "We're done in here. Let's go see how much too big it is. We always get one that looks just right, but when we get it in the house, it's a foot or so too tall."

When they walked into the living room Elizabeth

saw what Heather meant. The tree reached the ceiling and then some. Travis lowered it and Jesse grabbed a tool and proceeded to chop off the top of the tree and trim it up.

"Not even a foot this year." Tim Cooper beamed like a proud father, his pride focused on the tree they'd cut down. "We did good, honey."

Angie wrapped an arm around her husband. "We did. And the hot chocolate is ready. Let's warm up and then we'll eat lunch."

Elizabeth started to follow the rest of the family, but when she turned, Travis hadn't moved. He stood next to the tree, eyes closed. She waited for him to open his eyes.

He'd taken off his hat and he held it behind his back. His heavy coat had been dropped on a hook at the door. He wore a blue plaid button-down over a gray thermal shirt. His jeans were faded and worn. She wondered if he ever wore a suit and tie, and she liked to think he didn't.

"Travis, you okay?"

He opened his eyes and smiled. "Of course. It's something I do every year. This is a good time to re-member what God has done for me. And it's a good time to remember to pray for the family that gave me up."

"Why is this a good time?" She studied his face, remembering that he was the cowboy who went from one woman to another. So where did this side of him come from, this side that thought about God in a way she never had?

Maybe that was the difference between the Coopers and her own family. Christmas meant something more to this family. It meant more than gifts and holiday lights. It meant more than getting away to someplace warm.

Christmas meant faith. It meant a cowboy who took time to thank God for bringing him here.

"Christmas is always a good time to think about what God has done in our lives." He reached for her hand. "It's a good time to think about His blessings and why He puts us where we are. He took the time to put that baby in a manger; for a reason, not by accident."

"So I'm in Dawson for a reason?" The words slipped out, unplanned, she didn't even know what she meant by the question.

"Everything is for a reason." He led her out of the living room but stopped in the doorway.

She looked up into eyes that smiled. "What?"

He looked up and she followed his meaningful stare to the door frame and the sprig of mistletoe. "I've been thinking about that little piece of mistletoe since we left the house this morning."

"Have you?" she whispered and then forced the words a little louder. "Have you?"

"I have." He let out a deep breath and leaned. "Because last night, I wasn't sure if what happened was real."

"Last night?" she whispered again. She had to stop that. It didn't do her any good to sound breathless, to feel breathless, as if she was waiting for something to happen.

She cleared her throat. "What do you mean?"

"We're going to get caught." He leaned closer. "And I don't care."

She thought she didn't care either. She just wanted him to kiss her already. She took a step toward him and closed her eyes. She had her own questions about that kiss, the one that had rocked her world by making her feel something she'd never expected to feel.

"Are you two going to stand out here all day?" Heather laughed after the words interrupted their moment. "Oops, sorry."

Travis shook his head. "With this family, a person has to move quick. And if we don't get in there, we'll miss out on lunch."

Elizabeth really didn't care if she got lunch. As wonderful as the roast smelled, as sweet as the chocolate hinted at being, the temptation of that mistletoe kept her standing in the doorway of the living room.

Travis touched her cheek and he winked. His blue-green eyes held hers captive. "You're beautiful. Even with this twig in your hair."

She reached up but he stopped her hand and pulled something from her hair. He held the tiny twig in his hand.

"How long has that been there?"

"Back in the field. You must have gotten snagged on a branch."

"And you're just now telling me?"

"It was cute." He tucked it back behind her ear and she pulled it loose. "We should go, but do me a favor, okay?"

"What's that?"

"Stay out from under the mistletoe unless I'm the one here to kiss you."

"I'll stay out from under the mistletoe." Period. End of story.

Travis followed Elizabeth down the hall to the dining room with its floor-to-ceiling windows that looked out over the fields. The long table that stretched down the center of the room had been set with his mother's best china. The two roasts were placed with all the fixings, one at each end of the custom-made table.

His family stood around the table, each at their place. They always sat at the same place. Today they had left a chair next to him, the chair where Heather normally sat. She had taken Blake's place next to Jesse. He glanced around, noticed the knowing smiles, the winks, a few giggles from his nieces and nephews.

Yeah, he'd been set up. Well, being the clown of the family, he knew how to deal with surprises and uncomfortable situations. Make the best of it had always been his philosophy.

He pulled out the seat next to his. "I think you're supposed to sit here."

"Am I?" She narrowed in on an empty chair near his mother.

"That's Jackson's chair. In case he shows up."

"I see." She sat down and he pushed her chair forward.

He liked to think he had been saved by faith. Today he was saved by a prayer. Actually, by his dad asking a blessing on the food. For a minute everyone forgot to stare at him, to shoot looks his way. Of course it wouldn't last.

"Elizabeth, when do you plan on going home?" Lucky asked as he passed potatoes.

"I'm not sure. I should go soon. I have a lot to do. I think I should go tomorrow."

"If you do, you'll miss the living nativity at Back Street. Of course, I'm sure they have plenty of nativities in St. Louis." Jesse passed homemade rolls. "Ours is pretty small by comparison."

"I'm sure it's wonderful."

"We have the most wonderful Christmas Eve services at Dawson Community Church." Mia threw in that piece of information. Travis shook his head and his sister only smiled and flipped long dark hair.

"Let's eat and not try to push Elizabeth. She's had her schedule thrown off by all of this and she probably has a lot to do at home." His mom ended the conversation and then smiled. "But you really can stay as long as you like, Elizabeth."

Travis groaned. It slipped out before he could stop it. More giggles erupted and Mia wadded up a napkin and tossed it at him.

"Way to be inconspicuous, Trav."

"I'm sorry, but you all are too much. I wouldn't blame her if she called a taxi right now and asked them to get her out of here as soon as possible."

"What? Are you saying we're frightening?" Jesse prodded.

"I'm saying it's crazy here and I wouldn't blame her if she put those hiking boots back on and headed down the road."

"Actually, I'm enjoying it here."

Her soft words yanked him off his high horse. "You've got to be kidding."

She laughed a little. "No, actually, I was thinking that I don't have anywhere to go for Christmas." She looked down at her plate. "That sounds a little piti-ful, but with my parents out of the country…"

"You love us so much you're just looking for an excuse to stay and be a Cooper for a week or two," Jesse chimed in, while Travis couldn't think of a thing to say except that he wanted her to stay a lot longer than a week or two.

But a guy couldn't say that to a woman he'd known for a few days. Not even at Christmas, when any-thing seemed possible.

"I think you should stay." His dad finally entered the conversation. "If for no other reason than the fact that I've never seen Travis speechless. And also because no one should be alone at Christmas."

"I'll make a few phone calls and if there's nothing pending in St. Louis, I'll stay."

Travis decided being speechless might be a good thing. If he opened his mouth, he'd probably shove his foot straight in and not be able to pull it free.

He'd done a lot of that in his life, but this time what he said mattered. He couldn't explain it, but the woman at his side mattered in a way that no woman ever had. So what he said counted.

"I'm going to put the lights on the tree." He had finished his meal while everyone else was busy talking.

His mom watched him, her expression soft, questioning. He shrugged and walked to the sink to rinse his plate. When he turned, Elizabeth stood next to him.

"Want help?"

He needed help, but he knew she didn't mean the question to be about his mental state. "There's pie for dessert."

"I'll save mine for later."

He leaned against the counter, they were alone in the kitchen and he remembered that he hadn't gotten to kiss her under the mistletoe.

Maybe next time.

"You know that they're in there plotting against us, right?"

She moved to stand next to him. If someone walked

in, they'd see the two of them side by side, backs against the counter.

"Yeah, I know. I'm a big girl. I can handle it."

"If you're sure. They can be pretty determined."

"I'm sure they can. So can I." She smiled up at him and he wanted to forget mistletoe and common sense.

"Yeah, okay, let's go find the lights. They should be in a plastic tub in the living room. We hauled everything down from the attic earlier."

He touched her back as they walked down the hall to the living room. And he didn't stop her under the mistletoe, not this time.

Travis stood on the ladder, draping long strands of lights over the feathery branches of the cedar tree. The room smelled like Christmas. A cinnamon candle burned on the mantel and the cedar tree blended with the scent.

"Hold the lights out and make a trip around the tree. I'll arrange the lights as you move." Travis looked down from his perch on the ladder. Elizabeth smiled up at him, at the way he wavered and held the ladder, barefoot and putting a little more weight on his left foot.

As they worked, she could hear the rest of the family in the kitchen. Dishes clanked, glasses clinked. Laughter and conversation were muffled by the long hallway and the walls between them.

"They'll back off eventually." Travis moved the

string of lights and she walked around the tree again. They were nearly to the bottom.

"It's okay, they're not bothering me."

"All done." Travis climbed down from the ladder. "You okay?"

"I'm fine, why?"

"You look a little blotchy."

She shrugged. "Maybe from the heat in here. It's warm, don't you think?"

"No, it isn't warm."

"Well, I'm fine." She handed him the end of the lights. "Do you plug them in now?"

"No, we already made sure they work. We'll decorate the tree and plug in the lights when everything is done. Let's find the nativity."

"Lead the way." She itched a little, especially around her throat. Hopefully she wasn't coming down with something.

Travis turned to look at her, and then he looked closer. He touched her cheek and pulled back her hair.

"Elizabeth, you need to sit down."

"Why?" Because she was itchy? And hot? "I'm probably just getting a cold."

"Hey, Jesse, get in here." Travis brushed a hand through his hair, not exactly making her feel calm about things. "Now!"

"Travis, I'm fine." But she wasn't. Her throat was getting itchier. Her eyes were starting to water. "Really, I am."

And then she fell, straight into Travis Cooper's waiting arms.

"Jesse, quick!"

She could hear boots pounding on tile and wood. She felt Travis lift her off the ground. She didn't want to miss out on decorating the tree. She wanted to see the nativity and listen as Tim Cooper read the story from the Bible, because that's what he did every year.

"Shh, you're fine." Travis laid her on the couch, stepping back as Jesse hurried to her side.

"Heather, get my bag out of the closet." Jesse had his hand on her wrist and he was talking, but from far away. "Elizabeth, are you allergic to anything?"

"I don't think so."

"Have you ever been around cedar?"

She tried to shake her head. "But it smells good."

She tried to draw in a deep breath and it hurt, it wheezed in her chest. She gasped, suddenly afraid, her heart racing.

"Yes, it does smell good, little sister. Let me listen to your breathing, okay? I'm going to sit you up and I want you to breathe deep."

Strong arms lifted her and cold touched her back. She shivered in the arms that weren't Jesse's. She leaned against a chest that included a heavily beating heart.

"Give me the EpiPen, Heather." Jesse's voice was deep and close to her ear. "Elizabeth, you're having an allergic reaction and I'm worried about your breathing. I'm going to give you a shot and get your airway open again."

The sting in her hip brought her eyes open again. Jesse smiled and winked.

"Ouch," she whispered.

"Yeah, but not breathing, more of an ouch." He placed the stethoscope on her back again. "Breathe deep for me, okay?"

"I'm trying."

"Good girl." He listened again. "Sounding a little better in there. I'm going to give you some Benadryl and I want to keep you on that, just to make sure this doesn't happen again."

"And we're going to get that cedar tree out of here," Angie Cooper informed them, coming to stand close to Elizabeth.

"No, you can't do that." Elizabeth struggled against Travis, trying to sit up and face the family that had gathered to watch her little show. "I'm fine, and really, the tree is your tradition."

"The tree isn't as important as your health." Angie sat on the couch next to her. "You're our guest and we want you healthy and happy. That tree is a thing. It's a tradition, but it isn't why we celebrate Christmas."

"But it's so beautiful. I'm just a visitor and I don't want my presence here to dampen your holidays. I can leave."

"Nonsense." Angie hugged her. "Elizabeth, you will learn that we Coopers take things as they come.

We're always open to change. And that tree is something we do as a family, but the most important thing isn't that tree. We celebrate Christmas because it is a day to remember the birth of a little baby who would be our savior. The tree can be replaced by one from the store. It's that simple."

"I happen to have a tree in the store shed that we used a few years ago when one of our foster children had cedar allergies." Tim Cooper was already pulling on his gloves. "And we'll put the cedar tree out front, lights and all."

Travis had walked away. Elizabeth searched for him, needing, for whatever reason, to see him. He stood nearby, tall and a little awkward with a worried expression on his face.

"She's probably going to sleep for a little while." Jesse looked around. "Does someone want to take her upstairs?"

Travis stepped forward but his mother stopped him. "I bet she'd like to stay down here on the couch so she doesn't miss all of the fun. Travis, can you get a blanket and pillow from the hall closet?"

"I'm really okay," Elizabeth protested.

Jesse shook his head. "Last time I checked, I'm the family doctor and you're the lady who didn't know she was going into anaphylactic shock."

"Is that what that was?" She wiped at her eyes. "I feel silly."

"Don't." Angie moved closer as Jesse stepped away from them. "I'm just glad Jesse was here."

"And Jesse is just glad he always carries an EpiPen. I knew that wasp allergy would come in handy." Jesse packed up his black bag, and then pulled out a box of Benadryl. "You are going to need to go to your family doctor and get a prescription for an EpiPen. In case this ever happens again."

"Forever?"

"Forever. Elizabeth, an allergic reaction without proper treatment can be fatal. We kind of like having you around."

Travis reappeared with a blanket and pillow. He unfolded the blanket and draped it over her, sighing a little as he knelt next to her, lifting her to put the pillow behind her head.

"My turn to take care of you." He kissed her brow and then whispered in her ear, "But make no mistake, I'm going to get you under that mistletoe."

She shivered and closed her eyes. He kissed her cheek and then he was gone, leaving her alone on the couch, wondering how she would ever walk away from this family, and the man who should be the last person she'd want so desperately to keep in her life.

Maybe it was their faith that drew her to them. Maybe she needed their faith. Maybe that was her reason for being here and maybe it had nothing to do with Travis.

She breathed deep and even though she hadn't planned on sleeping, it happened.

Chapter Eight

Travis climbed the ladder and placed the star on a pretty decent-looking artificial tree. Most of the decorations had been hung. The lights had been turned on. The only things left to do were the candy canes and a few other decorations. Those had been saved for Elizabeth. She'd been asleep for two hours.

He stepped down off the ladder and walked over to the nativity that his nieces and nephews had set up on the coffee table. The tiny, hand-carved scene had always been his favorite Christmas decoration. It meant more to him than the tree. It meant more than the cookies the women were baking.

The nativity represented everything he believed about his faith. Without it, Christmas wouldn't be. All of his rebellious teen behavior would still be in him. There wouldn't be redemption.

The nativity scene had something that made it unique. The support beam of the stable looked like a rough, wooden cross. Yeah, that part always got him. From the tiny baby in a manger to the man who gave his life on the cross.

The whole story of salvation.

"Uncle Travis, are you going to cry this year?" Jacob, only five, looked up and asked.

"Of course not."

"Looks to me like he might cry," a sweet, soft voice commented.

He turned, surprised to see Elizabeth awake. Her face was flushed from sleep, her eyes were bright. She smiled up at him.

"I've been watching them, listening as they tell the story to each other."

"Yeah, that's what we do."

"I love your family." She brushed a hand through her hair. "I know a lot of people, Travis. None of them would have taken me in and then changed everything for me."

He sat down on the edge of the couch. "Of course someone would."

"No, not really." She sat up, wiping at her eyes with the edge of the blanket he'd placed over her earlier. "I'm sorry, I didn't mean to do that."

"If it makes you feel better, I do think my family is pretty terrific." He studied her face. "You're okay?"

"I am. I feel a little silly, but I'm okay. When we were in the field I started feeling a little itchy. I didn't think anything about it."

"I noticed." He smiled down at her. "I thought I might have to do CPR."

"Not on your life, cowboy."

He needed to go but he didn't want to leave, not yet.

"I missed out on the tree." She stared past him in the direction of the new tree. "It's beautiful, but I'll miss the cedar."

"Yeah, I won't miss your throat swelling shut. We saved some decorations for you."

"Thank you." She reached up, resting her hand on his cheek.

He didn't know what to say. He covered her hand with his and moved to kiss her palm. "I have to go."

"Of course."

The words cut into him and he didn't know why or exactly what she meant by them. He knew that he needed to get fresh air and think about this woman and how quickly she'd turned his life upside down. He needed to get a serious hold on reality because she didn't seem real.

"I'll let Mom know that you're awake. I'm going out to the barn."

"You don't have to. I'll go find everyone." She sat up, putting bare feet on the rug next to the sofa. Her brown eyes were liquid caramel in a pale face.

"You should rest."

"I've been resting." She stood up, leaning a little. "I'm fine."

"Okay. I'll see you later."

He looked back as he walked out the front door. Elizabeth had knelt and was talking to his nieces and nephews. They were showing her the baby Jesus and the star. They explained the angels and the shepherds. They pointed to the cross.

He walked out the front door and inhaled a deep breath of cold, Oklahoma air. He stood on the front porch and stared out at the field. The horses grazed in a close group, tails to the north, against the wind. What he'd like right now is to saddle his horse and go for a long ride.

Instead he headed for the barn and evening chores.

As he walked, the shepherd mix they'd had for about five years trotted up to his side. The dog barked and grabbed Travis's wrist. "Mooch, you have to stop doing that. You'll scare the city girl."

Mooch barked again and ran ahead of him to track something in the thick grass around the barn. Probably just a mouse. And the dog didn't stand a chance of actually tracking it down. Travis had come to the conclusion that the dog had no sense of smell. It had been sprayed by a skunk more than once. That didn't happen to a smart dog.

"Hey, you going to feed the cattle?" His dad walked out the side door of the barn. The double doors were closed against the cold north wind. They kept very few horses inside. Most were on pasture and had a shelter for bad weather. There were two studs and a couple of mares that they kept up. The stallions had runs with tall reinforced fencing. The mares were close to foaling and were kept in the corral during the day and inside at night.

They were careful with new foals at the Cooper Creek Ranch. Those babies were worth a lot of money.

"Yeah, I can feed. Is the truck parked out back?" Travis grabbed keys off a hook inside the barn.

"It is. I already loaded feed and there's a bale of hay on the spike."

"Gotcha."

His dad walked up, hat low over eyes that saw too much sometimes. Tim Cooper had lived a lot of life; he'd made mistakes and he'd made things right. Travis had nothing but respect for his dad. Biological or not, that's what Tim Cooper was to him, a dad.

"If you need to talk, I'm here." Tim pulled a pack of gum out of his pocket and offered Travis a stick.

"I'm good."

"I know you are. But I also know that look. I haven't seen it in you before, but I've seen it in Blake once. And in Lucky. Even Jeremy had that look."

"What look would that be, sir?"

Tim slapped him on the back. "You look like a man that's been bit."

"Nope, not that I know of. But I'm going to get those cattle fed so I can get to practice at Back Street."

"You can't run from it, Travis. You can get away by yourself and think, but you're going to have to deal with this."

"Yes, sir."

Deal with it. Yeah, he'd do that. He'd find a way to deal with a woman who had landed in his life, tied his heart up in knots and before would long hightail it out of Dawson. Which should be fine with him. He'd never lasted more than a few weeks in a relationship. And he'd tried. A year or so ago he'd tried real hard to make himself want to stay in a relationship with a woman from Tulsa.

Because he wanted to be married. He wanted kids and he wanted his own family traditions.

He started the flatbed farm truck, shifted into First and headed out through the field. Even though the temperature had dropped, he lowered the window. The dog barked and ran after the truck.

"In the back, Mooch."

Mooch slowed, circled and jumped on the back of the truck. Travis looked in the rearview mirror and watched the dog balance on the bags of feed.

Out here, alone, it was a lot easier to get his head on straight. Out here he could get his thoughts together. He breathed in. The air carried the scent of wet grass and snow.

Yeah, out here he could pray, really pray. That's what he did when he fed the cattle. He prayed as he dropped the bale of hay. He prayed as the cattle followed him to the feed trough. He had meant to flirt with Elizabeth, the way he always flirted. He figured she'd either brush him off or flirt back. He figured she'd be gone in a day or two, back to her life in St. Louis. No harm, no foul.

He hadn't expected to want to help her find faith. He really hadn't expected the strange tightening in his heart. It had started when she put on that Mrs. Claus costume. And he'd never believed in Santa. Living the first five years of his life in an orphanage, Santa hadn't been a part of his childhood.

He stopped at the feed trough, followed by a few dozen head of cattle. Mooch pushed the cattle back, barking and nipping at hooves as Travis poured grain in the trough. He stepped back and whistled. The dog turned and sat down next to him.

"Yeah, buddy, I couldn't imagine living anywhere but here."

Mooch, as if he really knew what Travis had said, barked a few times. Travis ruffled the fur at the dog's neck.

He whistled again and Mooch hopped in the open door of the truck and sat on the passenger side, tongue hanging out, lapping up the cold air from the open window.

Travis shook his head and got in the truck. "I can't say that I have any answers, Mooch. But I have one thing figured out. This isn't going to be easy."

Mooch looked at him, dark eyes all serious, like he really got it.

"Yeah, buddy, I remember that collie of Beth's showing up here. You were kind of in love, too, weren't you?"

He stopped the truck. Yeah, he'd just said love. He whistled long and low and shook his head. So this is what it felt like. No wonder people got a little crazy when it happened.

* * *

Elizabeth had ridden to Back Street with Heather. The two of them had helped get the cast for the living nativity into their costumes and then Heather had hurried off to the stable, where she had a part as a shepherd. They'd asked Elizabeth to put on a costume and join them. She'd explained that she couldn't. What if she had to go back to St. Louis?

As the cast went through the rehearsal, complete with Mary on a donkey and shepherds watching sheep, Elizabeth moved toward the stable so she could watch.

Even though she didn't mean to search for him, she found herself looking for Travis. He'd showed up just moments before the practice, late as usual. That's what Heather had called out to him as he hurried into the building to put on his costume.

Mary and Joseph had entered the inn. They would be turned away, of course, because there was no room in the inn. Elizabeth knew the story. She'd heard it. She'd probably read it a long time ago. Once upon a time her family had gone to a large church in St. Louis, before Harden Industries had grown to the point that it required more traveling and caused her father to work longer and longer hours.

Once upon a time she remembered being a child who sat on her father's lap, listening to him read the Christmas story.

She couldn't remember when they'd stopped that tradition. Had it meant more to her parents than a mere tradition or had it only been something that was easy to let go of?

Mary and Joseph left the inn, unable to find a room. She wondered why God couldn't have allowed the child to be born in a building, a real home. Instead Mary moved on to the stable, surrounded by animals.

Elizabeth stepped close, watching as Mary and Joseph made a place for themselves in the straw, surrounded by animals. God became man, someone spoke. She shivered at the words and watched as Mary put her newborn baby in the manger. For God so loved the world He gave His only son.

She could hear the words from her past, trickling back into her mind.

The shepherds watched over their sheep. One of the shepherds was Heather. She moved easily in her gray robe, keeping the lambs together. And suddenly a bright light shone round about and there was a multitude of the heavenly host—in costume—praising God and saying, Glory to God in the highest and on earth, peace, good will to men. For unto you is born this day, in the city of David, a savior who is Christ the Lord.

And this shall be a sign unto you…

Elizabeth turned and there, lying in the manger was the baby Jesus.

She pulled her coat a little tighter as the chill swept down her spine. For a moment she'd gotten lost in the pageant, almost felt as if she were there, in Bethlehem. A hand touched her arm. She jumped a little and turned, looking up in the blue-green eyes of Travis he watched next to her.

"This is the part I love," Travis whispered close to her ear. "I love when the shepherds, just quiet, humble men, are brought to the throne of God."

"To the stable, you mean."

"But look at where they are—the birthplace of a savior. We bow down and worship, at the feet of Jesus. Have you heard the song?"

She shook her head. She hadn't.

"These humble shepherds are bowing down at the feet of Jesus. They're humbled and in awe. Think about those angels appearing in the sky that night. I don't know, but I think I would have been so afraid, I wouldn't have been able to move. And when I finally did, I would have wanted to get to this spot, this stable, as quickly as possible."

"I remember my dad reading the Christmas story. And then we let go of those times and our lives became complicated, full of places to go and things to do."

"That happens. But remember, it isn't about the tree."

She smiled through her tears, remembering what Angie Cooper had said about the tree not being the reason they celebrate. The tree was part of tradition, but the celebration is about Jesus.

A light flashed in the night and the star lit up, illuminating the place where the baby Jesus slept.

"I've never..." She choked on the words.

His arm slid around her and he pulled her close to his side.

"It's okay." He kissed the side of her head and she nodded, and then she walked away.

She didn't know how to find her way to that baby, to the stable or that star. How did it become more than tradition? How did it become real, the way it seemed so real to the Coopers?

A thought whispered into her heart. Just ask. Ask God to make it real in her heart, in her life. Could it be that simple?

Angie Cooper looked up when Elizabeth walked down the steps and into the kitchen. She opened a bag of cookies and arranged them on a tray.

"Can I help you?" Elizabeth went to the sink and washed her hands. When she turned, Angie handed her a cup of coffee.

"I wondered the same thing, honey. Can I help you?"

"I don't know what you mean."

"Mascara. It's always a dead giveaway." Angie handed her a napkin.

"I'm sorry. You know, I'm not usually like this."

"You don't have to explain. And you can help me. I'm going to start pouring cherry punch in those paper cups. You can do that for me."

Elizabeth picked up the pitcher of red liquid and started filling the cups. "I'm curious about something."

"What's that?"

"I think I've always considered myself a Christian. But I don't really know."

Angie put down the container of cookies and took the pitcher from Elizabeth. And then she hugged her tight.

"Elizabeth, it's about what's in your heart. It's about what you know is true and accepting it as the truth."

The two of them stood in the quiet of the kitchen and Angie Cooper explained the truth about faith to Elizabeth, and when the cast and crew of the nativity came down the stairs thirty minutes later, the two of them were still crying as they ate cookies and drank coffee.

Angie walked away from her when Travis approached. He looked her over, as if he thought maybe she'd been hurt. But she hadn't been hurt. Maybe, for the first time in her life, she'd been made whole. She explained that to him and he pulled her into his arms.

The room grew strangely quiet as he lowered his lips to claim hers in the sweetest kiss ever. In the last hour her life had changed, taken new and startling turns. Those changes included a changed heart that was pieced back together.

Thirty minutes later it unraveled as she walked to the closet to retrieve her coat and over heard a conversation about herself and Travis.

Voices floated from a back room, saying Travis would break her heart because she looked like someone wanting a wedding ring and Travis had never been a long-term kind of guy.

People talked. She knew not to listen. But maybe she needed a reminder that just weeks ago she'd been planning her wedding.

Another broken heart was the last thing she needed for Christmas.

Chapter Nine

Travis woke up feeling pretty great. That's why he hurried through his chores, including watching a new foal come into the world, and then made his way up to the main house. He had a list of things to get done and he figured it would make Elizabeth pretty happy to know that he planned on buying gifts for the kids.

"Hey, where is everyone?" He walked through the house, smelling coffee but not hearing a sound. "Mom?"

"In here." She walked out of the office, not smiling.

"Where's Elizabeth?"

His mom sighed and pointed into the office. It was empty, so she obviously wanted him to sit down. This was the part where she gave him the bad news. It would have been nice to feel a little dread when he woke up, a little warning of impending doom. Instead he'd whistled like everything was going his way.

"I don't have time for long talks or to sit down. I

have a long list for the Samaritan House and a longer list for the community center. I'm a big boy. Shoot straight from the hip."

"She left this morning. Blake was heading into Tulsa and she needed to get a flight back to St. Louis. Something happened with their business and she was the only one available to take care of it."

Two nights ago he'd held her after she'd found faith. Last night they'd gone to the Mad Cow and he'd kissed her good-night. Today she had left without saying goodbye. Maybe this time he'd been the one who thought they'd had something that wasn't there.

"Is she coming back?"

"To be honest, I don't think she is."

"Good to know." He started down the hall toward the kitchen. His mom caught up with him, her hand reaching for his arm.

"Travis, it's okay to hurt."

"I'd rather not."

"Why?"

"Because it doesn't matter. She's just someone I've known for a week, nothing more." Obviously. "She has a home and a life in St. Louis."

His mom's hand rested on his shoulder. "I know. And I know that sometimes when you're hurt, you pretend you aren't. I don't know if this will help, but she was hurting, too."

"Yeah, there's not a lot I can do about that."

"Isn't there?"

"No, there isn't." He sipped his coffee and waited for the right words. He didn't know if there were any. "I'm not going to be the next guy to hurt her."

"Did you ever stop to think that you might be the one who wouldn't hurt her?" His mom, she always thought the best of her brood. He hugged her and then he walked away.

"Mom, I wish we could all believe in ourselves the way you believe in us."

"Maybe I see who God meant for you to be."

He stopped at the door and smiled at her. "Thanks for wanting a kid from Russia."

"I love you, Trav."

"Me, too, Mom. I'm going on into Tulsa. I'm going to get this shopping done and then I'll stay a few days and play Santa on Friday before Christmas."

"Trav, think about going after her. If she's the person you think might be the one, then don't let her get away. Let her know that you can be the man she needs you to be."

"What if I can't?"

"You already are."

Right, he was that man. If he was, he needed to convince Elizabeth Harden of that fact. But he had other priorities this close to Christmas. He had a list of items for kids in Dawson and a list for the kids at Samaritan House.

While he took care of his lists, he would think about how to bring Elizabeth back to Dawson for Christmas.

Back to him.

* * *

Elizabeth stood in the center of her apartment, trying hard not to think about unopened gifts, the wedding dress hanging in her closet. And the man she'd left in Dawson.

She'd stopped thinking about the man who'd left her.

Because he'd never been hers. Richard had never been in her heart, the person she couldn't imagine living without.

And she realized now that when he told her they were over, that there wasn't going to be a wedding, she'd been hurt, really hurt by his betrayal. She'd also been relieved and felt guilty about that emotion. By walking away he'd saved her from a future with a husband who didn't really love her, who wouldn't be faithful.

He'd saved her from marrying a man she didn't love.

So what did she have? An apartment full of wedding gifts that would have to be returned, an answering machine with messages from people asking if she'd made it home, did she want to attend a Christmas party, and saying how sorry they were about what happened.

She pushed the button and erased them all. On the way home from the airport she'd picked up a half gallon of butter pecan ice cream. She planned to eat the entire thing and try to figure out why she'd left Dawson.

Oh, she remembered. She'd panicked. When Travis had kissed her she'd panicked because she'd already been hurt, recently hurt. And he could hurt her again.

A knock on the door interrupted her thoughts. She'd panicked. She'd packed her bags because that kiss at the Back Street Church had changed things. He'd gone from temporary distraction to someone she could imagine in her life forever.

She peeked through the peephole and then unlocked the door to let her neighbor Mrs. Golden in. Sixty and retired, Mrs. Golden had nothing but time to watch what was going on in their hall.

"Well, now, it's about time you got back. I was afraid you'd run off to parts unknown." Mrs. Golden handed her a stack of mail. "I got your mail, just like you asked."

"Thanks, Mrs. Golden. And no, it really was just Oklahoma."

"A business trip, so soon after, well, you know?"

"No, not really. I stepped in for my dad at a charity bull riding event and then got delayed due to the storm."

Mrs. Golden smiled big. "Oh, bull riding. I do love cowboys. Mr. Golden grew up on a ranch. That was a long time ago and he's been gone longer. Well, we won't talk about that. But did you meet a good-looking cowboy while you were there?"

"There were quite a few cowboys." She flipped

through her mail, dropping junk mail into the trash can next to the door.

"Oh, goodness."

Elizabeth looked up. "What?

"You fell in love. I can see it in your eyes. Oh my, is he handsome?"

"Mrs. Golden, I was gone only a week. That isn't time to fall in love."

"Of course it is. Sometimes a heart just knows."

"Does it? I thought I was in love before."

"Sweetie, you didn't have that look in your eyes when you were engaged to that young man. Sometimes love just happens."

"Yes, but sometimes it isn't love. Sometimes it's just…"

"What?"

Elizabeth looked down at her mail, wishing she hadn't opened the door to her nosy but well-meaning neighbor. For some reason she always felt compelled to talk to Mrs. Golden. She'd shared a lot with the lady in the five years they'd been neighbors.

"What if he's like Richard?"

Mrs. Golden shrugged. "Honey, what if he isn't? What if he's as in love with you as you are with him, and you'll never know because you ran off and didn't give it time. If your heart is breaking at the thought of never seeing him again, then I'd say you'd better give me that key to your mailbox and get yourself a flight back to Tulsa."

Elizabeth laughed a little. "I'll think about it."

Mrs. Golden, gray-haired and slim, patted her cheek. "You do that. Now I'm going to go and let you think about what you're going to be doing for Christmas."

Christmas. She closed her door and walked into the living room. No tree. No decorations. No Christmas gifts.

Gifts. The children at Samaritan House. But of course Travis would take care of them. He would buy their gifts. He would play Santa for them.

She would miss out. Her heart ached at the thought. It ached to think of spending Christmas here alone. Especially when she thought about the nativity. She would miss watching it at Back Street Community Center.

So what should she do? Put her heart on the line? Risk being hurt again?

She picked up her mail and a postcard fell out. From her parents. They were having a great time and hoped she was doing okay. They encouraged her to do something for Christmas, not just sit in the apartment but go somewhere or at least stay with friends.

Yes, friends, like the Coopers, a family she hadn't known until last week. She smiled, remembering the tree they'd taken down. For her. And now she'd left and they didn't have their traditional tree.

Her phone rang. She looked at the caller ID and recognized the Oklahoma area code. She let it ring, let it go to voice mail. And then she walked into the bathroom with her fluffy robe.

But she could hear the message from the answering machine. It was Heather's voice asking if Elizabeth would be back for Christmas.

"What do you want her to think about you?" Uri asked Travis as the two of them sat in the dining room of the bed-and-breakfast. "And most important, why is she different?"

"I want her to realize that I'm a man who is worthy of her. I want her to realize that I'm a man who will stay in her life. When I'm with her, I don't think of moving on. I think of settling down. And I think of tomorrow with her, and the next day and the day after."

His uncle laughed. "Sounds like love, if you want the opinion of an old man."

"I wanted your opinion. That's why I'm here." Travis stood up, stretching to relieve the kinks from sitting too long. "But I'm still not sure what to do. She's been hurt and I'm sure she's thinking that I'll hurt her, too."

Uri poured himself another cup of coffee from the carafe on the table. "You've created a reputation for yourself, Travis. Sometimes a man has to prove his mettle."

"Yeah, I guess that's true. But it will have to wait. As much as I want to jump on a plane and fly to St. Louis, I can't. I have a group of kids waiting for gifts and winter coats. And I have people expecting me back home tonight for the living nativity."

"You'll work this out." Uri stirred sugar into his coffee. "And I know you'll pray about it. You can't drag someone into your life just because you want them there. If this relationship is what God has for you, then let God bring it all together."

Travis sat back down. "I've known her less than two weeks. I can't imagine that it's love. It's just that she changes me. When I'm with her..."

"I know, you feel like a better man."

"Well, I'm not sure I would have said that, but okay."

"If you want to be a better man for her sake, then I think it's time you stop and think that it might be love. At least give it a chance."

"Thanks, Uri. I should go now. I've got everything loaded in the truck."

"Where's your Santa suit?"

"In the truck. I left the Mrs. Claus costume at Samaritan House. I guess we won't need it this year." It wasn't as if they'd ever had a Mrs. Claus. The kids were used to his showing up alone.

"Maybe next year there will be a Mrs. Claus. And if it isn't Elizabeth Harden, well, at least you know that when the right woman comes along, you'll know it."

"Right, I'll know it."

A few minutes later he pulled up to Samaritan House. He backed up the driveway to make it easier to unload the truck. As he cut the engine the garage door opened. He glanced in his rearview mirror and smiled at Dutch who had walked out through the garage.

"Hey, Dutch." Travis got out of the truck, grabbing the Santa suit on the way out. "Are the kids excited?"

"Oh yeah, they're excited. Where's Mrs. Claus? They were looking forward to seeing her again."

"Yeah, bad news on that. She's back in St. Louis."

And he'd let her go. He'd been thinking about that a lot. He'd been thinking he should hightail it up to St. Louis and tell her she couldn't walk out on a Cooper, not without a real good reason. Especially when that Cooper thought he might be in love for the first time ever.

"I wouldn't let that one get away, Travis." Dutch grabbed a couple of the big boxes from the back of the truck. "Man, this is a lot of stuff."

"Gloves, coats, snow boots and toys. We really did great this year, Dutch. We got everything on their list."

Dutch shook his head. "I don't know what we'd do without you, Travis. That new heating system you all put in is making a real difference."

"That's what Christmas is all about, Dutch. If we aren't showing a little love, His love, then what in the world are we doing calling ourselves Christians? There isn't much in this world I want or need, so why buy myself more or ask for more? But these kids, they need everything and they didn't ask for much at all."

"They're great kids, Travis. They fill this big old house up with laughter and love."

Travis grabbed a couple of huge bags and followed Dutch into the garage.

"Let's leave it out here. Jemma can sort it out."

"We've got it sorted. Now the coats and such, that you can sort out, but the gifts are in individual bags inside the big bags."

"I've never known you to be so organized, Travis." Dutch opened the bags and peered in. He whistled. "You did real good."

"Yeah, I just thought it would be easier this way. I've spent the last couple of days getting it all together and organized."

And thinking about Elizabeth. He hadn't stopped thinking about her. Another reason why he needed to talk to her.

"Let's grab a cup of coffee before you change into your costume."

"That sounds good." Travis followed him up the steps and into the house. "Is that chocolate chip cookies I smell?"

"I think it might be. The kids have been making Christmas cookies today, too." Dutch slipped off his coat and hung it in the hall closet. "Did you want to go in there and change into your costume?"

Travis shrugged, "Yeah, I guess I can."

"I'll meet you in the kitchen."

Travis walked down the hall a few minutes later, decked out in his red suit, boots clomping on the floor. Yeah, true, none of the kids were fooled by the costume. He doubted any of them believed in Santa, and they definitely knew that Christmas was about the birth of Jesus. But the Santa gig had become tradition. It was fun for him, fun for the kids. If it made them smile, he'd do it forever.

The smell of chocolate chip cookies lured him to the kitchen and he stopped short in the doorway, forgetting about the mouth-watering smells, forgetting that he was dressed in red velvet. He forgot pretty much everything, maybe even his name.

Because Mrs. Claus was standing in the kitchen, her cheeks pink, her hair tucked up in the red-and-white bonnet. Her brown eyes flickered and sparkled with moisture. She whispered, "Hello, Santa. I hope you don't mind. It was lonely up north."

"I don't." He cleared his throat. "I didn't know. When did you get here?"

She smiled a sweet smile and stepped closer. "Yesterday. I stayed here last night."

"You were here? Last night?"

She nodded. "I was. You see, my family doesn't have a lot of Christmas traditions and I decided to make a few of my own. Most of them have to do with Oklahoma."

"I see. I take it you're planning on spending Christmas here?"

She bit down on her bottom lip and nodded again.

"I think I plan on spending Christmas at Cooper Creek, if that's okay."

"I think that's more than okay. How long do you plan on staying?" Out of the corner of his eye he saw Dutch and Jemma leave the room, and they were alone, he and Elizabeth.

Elizabeth had worried he'd be upset. She'd thought this through, kind of. She'd thought about it enough to know that her heart could be broken if he didn't want her here. But he wasn't upset, he was smiling. He stepped closer, close enough to touch.

"I think I might stay for a while." She looked down at the ground and when he touched her chin, raising it with a finger, she smiled.

"A while?"

She nodded. "There's this cowboy that I kind of like. He's cute in a red Santa suit and he thinks I make a pretty decent Mrs. Claus. A few days ago I got scared, thinking he might not like me as much as I like him. And then I decided that it would be wrong to stay away, to not take a chance."

"I'm glad you're willing to take a chance because the cowboy in mind is pretty crazy about you. He felt his own heart break a little when you left."

"Really?"

"Really. Because for the first time in his life, in my life, I think I've met someone who makes me think about settling down."

"I love you, Travis." She stood on tiptoe and kissed his cheek.

He whispered that he loved her back and then she was in his arms, no regrets. His hands held her close and his lips touched hers, promising so much. He moved, his mouth hovering and then returning. "Elizabeth, I love you."

Little feet pitter-pattered down the hall. Elizabeth stepped back, running her hands down her sides to smooth the Mrs. Claus suit. But her eyes were locked with the eyes of a guy who played the cutest, skinniest Santa she'd ever seen.

Then suddenly they were surrounded by children. Christmas had never meant as much as it meant at that moment. She and Travis already had their tradition.

Most of all, they had each other. And she knew that he would always be her Christmas cowboy.

* * * * *

Dear Reader,

It's Christmas in Dawson. Join the Coopers for a season of tradition, love and faith. In *Her Christmas Cowboy,* the heroine, Elizabeth Harden, learns a valuable lesson about love and loss. She also learns that traditions aren't as important as the faith behind those traditions.

When it comes to Christmas, the folks in Dawson understand the real meaning behind the season. Celebrate with them as they celebrate the birth of a savior.

Merry Christmas!

Brenda Minton

Questions for Discussion

1. Elizabeth Harden expected to be one place for Christmas but she finds herself in the place she least expected to be. Would faith have helped her to handle the situation differently? Or did she handle the upset as well as expected?

2. Travis Cooper has always been rowdy and a little high-strung. He has faults, as we all do. How does accepting help him to be a better person?

3. Elizabeth expected to go home to her empty apartment. That was her plan. How do her plans change and how will that change her life?

4. Angie Cooper explains to Elizabeth that the cedar tree the family brings into the home is just part of tradition, it can be replaced. What can't be replaced and what is the real focus of Christmas for the Coopers?

5. How do traditions help the family to celebrate?

6. What does Elizabeth learn about herself during the living nativity?

7. In helping the children at Samaritan House, what does Travis learn about himself?

8. How does Elizabeth take control of her own life to find where she needs to be?